Lammas Publishing

This book is dedicated to my husband Clive, in love and gratitude.

This story is set in actual places, Dunoon, York and Bungay. The hospital and ferries exist, but imaginative liberties have been taken concerning their layout and activities within. The military base and all other buildings are fictional. All characters are fictional and not based on any individual, living or deceased.

1

I, Dr Maud, live in Dunoon, a small town on the Cowal Peninsula off the west coast of Scotland, where ocean tides wash back and forth into sea lochs. The road on which my bungalow sits curves up the hillside from the A815 coast road. My living room looks out on the Clyde estuary as it flows down from Glasgow to the Atlantic Ocean. Across the estuary I can see the entry to Gare Loch, but the submarine base at Faslane on the eastern shore is not visible from my window, although I do occasionally see a submarine entering or leaving the Loch. They turn up unexpectedly, and I dare say their movements, and indeed everything about them, is a closely-guarded secret.

There is a bus stop on the coast road opposite my bungalow. The bus passes the car ferry terminal on its way to the town. The ferry takes us across to the mainland at Gourock in just twenty minutes, saving a sixty mile drive round by road. From there we are only 25 miles west of Glasgow, Scotland's largest city, and are thus connected by road, rail, air or cruise ship to the rest of the world. For local transport I also have a twenty some-year-old blue Beetle. It has been gently used and, despite comments from various quarters, is nowhere near its sell by date. These seemingly mundane facts all played a part in the drama which began to unfurl one Monday afternoon last summer.

The weather was fine, no need to use the car, so I walked into town to pick up a few groceries from the supermarket and took the bus home. A perfectly normal day so far. I put my shopping down on the ground while I dug my house key out of my purse. As I did so I noticed a flat package stuffed into the little alcove I have by the door. I didn't think twice about it because I often order books on the web and have a standing arrangement with our local carriers and the postman to leave parcels that won't go through the letter box in the alcove when I'm not home.

I hadn't ordered anything on line recently but my twin sister Gabriella, an inveterate handcrafter, sometimes sends me things she has made, so I assumed this particular one would be from her. It was fairly small, and judging by the shape it was probably another painting of flowers she'd grown in her garden. I have quite a collection of them. Curious anyway to see what masterpiece she had sent this time, I picked up the package to take indoors, and it was then that I noticed it was not addressed to me. In clear black letters, obviously written with a felt pen, it was addressed to a Captain John Walker, but at my postal address. Obviously someone had made a mistake and I needed to arrange for it to be returned. I put it down on the table by the front door where I normally put letters ready for posting, and telephoned the carrier to come by and collect it on his rounds next morning. I never gave it another thought at the time. Maybe I should have.

2

The following morning, Tuesday, the doorbell rang. It was the carrier.

'I've come for the package you called about yesterday, Dr Maud. The one you said had your address but wasn't for you.'

'Yes of course, I have it right here waiting for you.' I smiled. 'Thank you for coming to collect it.'

But then, when I looked down at my hall table the package wasn't there. That was very odd. I distinctly remembered putting it there the previous day before I called the carrier. I looked under the table in case it had fallen. No package there either, or anywhere else in the hallway.

'I'm awfully sorry,' I told him, 'I was so sure I put the package on the table yesterday, ready for you to pick up. Would you mind waiting a minute while I see if I left it in the kitchen?'

A quick scan of the kitchen counters revealed no package. I went back to the carrier apologetically.

'I'm just mortified,' I told him. 'I must have put the darned thing down somewhere but I just don't see it anywhere.'

'Did someone come by to pick it up already?' he suggested.

His question worried me. Was I getting forgetful, as my sister recently hinted? Had someone actually been to collect it and I'd forgotten? My face must have registered my anxiety.

'Don't worry about it Dr Maud,' the carrier said gently. 'Just call and let me know when you find it.'

For the next half hour I searched the house for that package. I checked in my food cupboards and in the refrigerator in case I had stashed it with the groceries. I looked in every room in the house in case I had picked it up and put it down somewhere without thinking. I was still searching when the telephone rang.

The voice was male and curt. He did not identify himself. 'You have a package that was sent to your house.'

I was still fretting about not being able to find it and so surprised by the call that I didn't think to question his motives. 'As a matter of fact,' I blurted out, 'I don't have it. A package was delivered here yesterday that was addressed to a Captain Walker but it doesn't seem to be here now. I put it on my hall table yesterday and it wasn't there this morning. So yes, I did have a package sent to my house, but I can't lay my hands on it now.'

It suddenly dawned on me that I had no

idea who I was talking to. Could this be the mysterious Captain John Walker? He hadn't said so. 'By the way,' I said, 'Who am I talking to?'

The line went dead.

The number registered on my caller ID was not a local one so I guessed the man was probably calling on a mobile. I decided not to call back. I had already given out far too much information without checking who I was speaking to. He could call again if he wanted to.

I decided not to worry about it. If the man on the telephone called back, he could tell me where to send it. Otherwise I would call the carrier when it eventually turned up and that would be the end of the matter. I made myself a cup of instant coffee and settled down with yesterday's Daily Telegraph crossword.

Half way through it, my train of thought was interrupted by the sound of mail being pushed through the letter box. I went to see what had arrived. It is rarely exciting, mostly bills or circulars, but I'm an optimist: it's always worth looking. I was in luck that day. My copy of the British Medical Journal had arrived and another magazine I had been expecting.

As I carried the magazines to my favourite chair in the living room a letter fell out from between them. I picked it up to see who it was from. To my consternation, like yesterday's package, it was addressed to Captain John Walker. There was no return address. Straight away, I went to find a black marker pen in my desk drawer and wrote firmly across the envelope in large, bold letters, 'Not known at this address.' I took the letter through into the hallway and put it on the table by the door where I would see it and remember to take it to the post box when I next went out.

I went back to my chair, finished the crossword and started to read the correspondence in the British Medical Journal, the part I always enjoy most. I was on the third letter when the doorbell rang. There on the doorstep stood a fresh-faced youth together with a bucket and a ladder.

'I'm cleaning windows along this street today, Ma'am. Can I do yours?'

'Well,' I told him, 'I already have a window cleaner. He comes every two weeks. He'll be here again next Monday.'

'I've just been looking at your windows, Ma'am. I don't think he does a very good job.'

I have to say that they looked fine to me but young people do need jobs and I did have neighbours coming round the following day. It wouldn't hurt to have them sparkling for the occasion.

'All right, go ahead and do them,' I told him. 'I imagine you charge the same as my regular man?'

'Er ... fine, but I'll need paying today, in cash.'

'Just ring the doorbell when you've finished.'

I did wonder why the young man had brought a ladder. Some of my windows are higher up because the house is built on a slope, but Hamish, my regular window cleaner, always uses a long squeegee extension to reach them. Still, I supposed, a ladder should do the job equally well. I went back indoors and settled once more to my BMJ.

The young window cleaner seemed to be taking much longer than Hamish but I wasn't concerned. It was only to be expected that someone unfamiliar with the house and using a ladder rather than a squeegee would be slower.

When the doorbell finally rang I went to answer it with the money in hand. I was very surprised to see a young woman standing there. She looked perhaps in her thirties with neatly cut blonde hair, designer jeans, a cream open neck shirt under a smart plaid jacket, and sandals with heels. The window cleaner was balancing his ladder alongside the window by the front door.

'Good morning,' I smiled at the young woman, 'can I help you?'

'I'm Mrs Walker, Captain Walker's wife,' she said hurriedly. 'I understand a package for my husband was sent here yesterday by mistake, and a letter for him probably arrived today as well. I've come to collect them both and to apologise to you for the inconvenience.'

'Well, Mrs Walker,' I responded happily, 'I'm certainly glad you came for them. I don't know why on earth Captain Walker's mail was sent here, but there's no need for you to apologise. In fact, I must apologise to you. I seem to have mislaid the package, but you can certainly take the letter. I was going to take it to the post box this morning anyway. I'll call you when the package turns up if you give me your telephone number.'

I turned to pick up the letter which I had put on the hall table less than half an hour ago. It had vanished. As before, I checked under the table to see if it had fallen, but to no avail. Was I really beginning to forget things? There had been no one else in the house, so both the package and the letter had to be somewhere.

I felt terribly embarrassed. How could I explain to Mrs Walker that I had somehow managed to mislay the letter as well as the package?

Then I heard a scuffling and a crash from outside the front door. I rushed out to see what had happened. Mrs Walker was lying on the ground with the window cleaner's ladder on top of her.

3

'I hope it didn't hit her too hard,' the window cleaner blurted out. 'I'm really sorry. The ladder slipped out of my hand. I think it hit her head. Do you think she's alright?'

Mrs Walker's head was bleeding badly. She was groaning and drifting in and out of consciousness.

'Get that ladder off her immediately,' I commanded, 'and prop it up somewhere safe while I take a look. She may be badly hurt. How on earth did it happen?'

He lifted the ladder off the woman. I crouched down beside her and checked her over quickly. The only obvious injury I could see was a deep gash on the side of her head where the ladder had made contact. On cursory examination she appeared to be otherwise unharmed. Some bruising might show up later as a result of falling onto the hard ground but my main concern was the head injury. I told the window cleaner to watch her while I went indoors for a temporary dressing to cover the wound.

'I'm going to drive her to A&E myself,'

I told him. 'It'll be quicker than waiting for an ambulance. Head injuries can be very serious and A&E can check the rest of her much more thoroughly on an examination table than I can out here. I'll just back the car out of the garage and you can help me get her into it. It won't take long to run her up the hospital, then I'll settle up with you when I get back.'

I hurried indoors, grabbed my purse and keys, opened the garage door and backed out. The young man and I half-walked, half-carried our patient to my blue Beetle and strapped her in.

Our local hospital is only a mile or so away and Mrs Walker was still woozy when we arrived. I drove right up to the door, snagged one of the waiting wheelchairs, and called for help. One of the hospital staff came out and helped me get her into the chair and wheeled her in while I parked.

Mrs Walker was on her way into the examination room when I arrived in reception. I was asked to describe what had happened. I identified myself as Dr Maud (retired) and told them how Mrs. Walker came to be standing outside my front door at the same time as the window cleaner. I explained that I was in the house looking for a letter at the time so I hadn't actually seen the accident happen, but I heard a crash, and then found Mrs Walker lying unconscious on the ground. According to the window cleaner, his ladder had slipped and struck Mrs Walker on the head. I told them that she had not fully recovered consciousness.

The nurse then directed her attention to her patient. She examined the head wound carefully, looked in her ears, checked her pupils, pulse and blood pressure, and looked for signs of damage elsewhere. By this time Mrs Walker was becoming a little more responsive and was able to follow the nurse's finger with her eyes when asked to do so.

'Now, can you tell me your name?' the nurse asked.

'Margaret Browne,' her patient replied drowsily. 'Browne with an 'e', and I go by Peggy.'

Fortunately the nurse was too intent upon her patient to notice my surprise.

'You go by your maiden name then, Peggy?'

I had originally identified her to the A&E staff as Mrs. Walker, of course.

'I'm not married.'

'So you're Peggy Browne, not Peggy Walker?'

'Yes. Why did you call me Peggy Walker?'

'Because the lady that brought you in said you were Mrs Walker.'

'Oh. No I'm Peggy ... my head hurts.'

'Do you know where you are, Peggy?'

Peggy's gaze travelled round the room. I quickly sidled round behind her head, out of her range of vision, before she could focus on me. I wanted to hear more about this woman who was not Mrs Walker at all, but a Miss Peggy Browne with an 'e'. She continued to gaze around.

'Is this a hospital?'

'Yes, you've been brought here because you've had an accident.'

'My head hurts.'

'Peggy, do you know where you live?'

'London ... I used to live in London ... with Dave now ... places ... places ...'

'Is Dave your boyfriend then?'

'Yes, Dave ... '

Dave indeed! Both the package and the letter had been clearly addressed to Captain John Walker not Captain Dave Walker. Peggy Browne with an 'e' was definitely not the Mrs Walker she claimed to be. The nurse continued,

'Did Dave bring you here, Peggy?'

'I don't know ... I don't think so. My head hurts.'

'Do you know where Dave is now, Peggy?'

'I'm meeting him at 11 o'clock ... what time is it?

'Don't worry about the time. You won't be meeting him at 11 o'clock today. I'm going to have the doctor look at you. He'll probably want to X-ray your head to see if you sustained a fracture and we may want to keep you here for a while for observation. But we can try to contact your boy-friend and tell him you're here. Where were you meeting him?'

'At the hotel.'

'Which hotel? Can you remember the name of the hotel?'

'Bell something.'

'The Bellevue Hotel?'

'Yes. My head really hurts.'

'You're staying at the Bellevue Hotel?'

'Yes.'

'Down by the water?'

'Yes.'

'And what's Dave's other name, Peggy, so that we know who to ask for when we call the hotel?'

'Smith. Dave Smith. My head still hurts.'

'Right, here's the doctor now.'

It was time for me to leave. I had done all I could for Peggy Browne with an 'e'. From now on her boyfriend Dave Smith could take over.

4

I sat in my Beetle in the hospital car park, thinking. The events relating to the disappearance of the package and letter had originally seemed unusual but nothing to be alarmed about. I could have mislaid both. After Mrs Walker a.k.a. Peggy Browne's injury with the ladder and her revelations in the hospital, I realised that the situation was rather more complicated. Taken separately, each event, even Peggy Browne's head injury, was unusual but could have been coincidence.

Collectively however, too many odd things had happened to be purely coincidental. I think best with a pen in my hand so I took out the notebook I keep handy in the glove compartment of the Beetle and made notes.

Package for Captain JohnWalker delivered yesterday

Package gone from hall table this morning

Man telephoned about package. Rang off when asked for ID

Letter for Captain John Walker arrived this morning

'Mrs Walker' came to house for husband's

mail

Letter no longer on the hall table either

Window cleaner's ladder fell on 'Mrs Walker'

'Mrs Walker' is Peggy Browne. Boyfriend Dave Smith

Nine coincidences? No way! Then I recalled Peggy Browne telling the nurse in A&E that she and Dave Smith were staying at the Bellevue Hotel and that she was meeting him there at 11 o'clock. I looked at my watch. It was already a quarter past eleven. I guessed he would probably still be there waiting for her. Maybe he could explain what was happening.

Without further ado I started my engine and drove down the hill to the shore road. I turned left and then left again into the courtyard of the Bellevue Hotel and backed into a parking slot conveniently opposite the hotel entrance. My plan was to try to catch Dave Smith before he left. If he was still at the hotel, he'd almost certainly be meeting Peggy in the hotel bar. I had no idea what he looked like, but I could easily go into the bar and look around. If I spotted a likely candidate I would think of an excuse to speak to him and find out if he was Dave Smith and if so, maybe I could tell from his voice if he had been my telephone caller. In fact, I could ask him directly.

I had one foot out of the car door when a taxi turned into the courtyard and stopped in front of the hotel entrance. I wondered if it had been called to take Dave Smith up to the hospital. I hastily pulled my leg back into the car, grabbed my map book and pretended to study it while I watched covertly from the car.

The taxi driver got out of his vehicle and went inside. He came out again carrying a couple of suitcases, closely followed by a woman carrying a baby, and a man carrying a folded push chair, a football and a child's scooter. They were followed by three children, a little girl cradling a doll, a little boy who immediately ran out into the courtyard veering from side to side with his arms outstretched making vroom-vroom noises, and another girl who looked about seven or eight years old still in the hotel entryway, trying unsuccessfully to rein in a small, barking dog on an expandable leash.

Amidst this turmoil, a second man, not part of the family group, came rushing out of the hotel. The dog, now thoroughly excited, danced round the newcomer, barking and showing its teeth. The leash wrapped itself around his legs and, as he tried to free himself, the handle of the leash was jerked out of the girl's hand and caught the boy on his leg. The human aeroplane became an angry little man.

'Daddy,' he yelled, 'Sally let go of the lead and it hit me. She did it on purpose.'

He charged at his sister. The father dropped the pushchair and toys he was carrying and rushed back to separate the two angry children.

'What the hell!' the entangled man yelled, arms waving, legs bound together by the leash cord, grabbing the door jamb to keep his balance. 'Can't anyone control this dog? Get out of the way, all of you!'

Calmly, the taxi driver walked over, picked the little dog up and unclipped the extended leash from its collar.

'You'll find it easier to get loose now, sir,' he said.

The family watched open mouthed as the man untangled his legs, threw the leash angrily to the ground and strode wordlessly to a black Vauxhall parked at the side of the courtyard. I observed him carefully from the vantage point of my car. Medium height, floppy black hair, maybe in his forties, jeans, open-neck red shirt, light brown leather windbreaker. Unfortunately I couldn't be sure about the voice because he had been shouting.

The courtyard was not large so the man with floppy black hair had to wait until the family were all loaded up and the taxi moved away before he could back his car out of its slot. I thought it unwise to approach the angry stranger so decided to watch and possibly follow him a little way to see if he was heading towards A&E. I waited until he was lined up to turn out onto the road before starting my own engine. An arrow on a road sign almost opposite the Bellevue Hotel indicated a right turn for the hospital. The black car turned left. Hmmm! Since I had to turn left to go home anyway I followed at a discreet distance. The black car turned right at the ferry dock and joined the queue for the next ferry to the mainland.

I could think of three possible explanations for the man driving straight to the ferry dock. First, my suspicions had been wrong and the man in the car was not Dave Smith after all. Second, maybe he was Dave Smith but the hospital had not succeeded in making contact with him and he got tired of waiting for Peggy. Third, maybe he was Dave Smith and on receiving the message that Peggy had suffered an injury and was at the hospital had decided discretion was the better part of valour and left her in the lurch.

Nothing else could happen that morning, could it? I drove home.

5

My conscience smote me as I turned into the driveway. I could see the window cleaner pulling weeds in my herbaceous border. I had forgotten all about him. I had taken off for A&E with the injured Mrs Walker, a.k.a. Peggy Browne with an 'e', without paying the poor lad. I hadn't reckoned on a wild goose detour via the Bellevue Hotel. His money was still in my pocket.

'Hello!' I called to him. 'I'm so sorry I kept you waiting all this time. I had your money all ready for you but forgot about it when the accident happened. Anyway, you'll be glad to know the woman's going to be all right. When I left the hospital they were taking her to X Ray and talking about keeping her there for observation. I'm sure she'll be all right though.'

I suppose I was expecting some expression of concern or even some sign of relief at this news but the young man just shrugged and looked sullen. I thought maybe I had upset his schedule by keeping him waiting. Wanting to make amends, I handed him the notes from my pocket then added,

'How about I give you a little more to make

up for keeping you waiting and also to thank you for pulling my weeds. I didn't ask you to do that but I'm certainly very grateful. Just wait a minute while I go indoors for it.'

I rushed inside without waiting for a reply. I didn't realise the window cleaner was following me until I got to the kitchen, where I keep loose change in a ceramic urn labelled 'cookie jar' for just such an occasion. Before I reached it I sensed a presence behind me. Turning, I found myself face to face with the young man.

'Where are they, Dr Maud?' he demanded impatiently.

I was annoyed by his rudeness. I assumed that by 'they' he meant more ten pound notes. I was unwilling to reveal my hiding place so decided to stall until I got him out of the kitchen.

'Young man,' I asserted my authority, 'I did not invite you into my house. Please wait outside.'

'Not until I get what I came for, Dr Maud.'

'Then you're going to have a long wait. I don't like rudeness. Anyway, how do you know my name?'

He ignored the question. 'Just get them for me and I'll go.'

'I've told you, wait outside.'

'Oh, all right.'

He left the kitchen and I heard his retreating footsteps through the hallway. I reached into my cookie jar. To my consternation the money had all gone, all the notes and loose change. I blazed out of the house.

'How dare you!' I shouted. 'You thief! You've been in my cookie jar and stolen the money that was there! I'm going to call the police.'

The window cleaner pushed me gently but firmly back into the house.

'Calm down, Dr Maud,' he soothed. 'I don't know what you're talking about. I haven't taken any money. All I want is the package that came here addressed to Captain John Walker.'

'What? What did you say?' I screeched, unable to believe my ears. 'Who are you?'

The young man drew himself up to attention. 'Special Branch,' he announced proudly.

'You look awfully young for such responsibility,' I said doubtfully. 'You're going to have to show me some ID.'

He dug into the back pocket of his jeans and waved a laminated card with his picture on it. I recognised it at once but decided to play along with the charade.

'There was a package delivered here yesterday for Captain Walker,' I told him cautiously. 'And a letter came for him this morning as well, but they both seem to have gone missing. I have no idea where either of them are.'

I heard the front door open and a second youth joined us.

'Hey Tony, it's not in her car either.'

The newcomer looked about the same age, and had the same generally untidy appearance as the window cleaner. He was wearing jeans and a jeans jacket. Like the other lad, he wore black trainers on his feet.

'Right, so she's the only one that knows where it is. Hey man,' the one called Tony said with a long look at the newcomer, 'it was you that searched this room. You took some money out of here, didn't you?'

'Sure, it was in that big pot over there that says 'cookies' on it.'

'Well put it back. That's not what we came for. We're not thieves, at least I'm not.'

'Hell Tony, we've earned it.'

'Put it back!'

The second youth reluctantly dropped notes and coins into the jar. Tony was clearly in charge.

'So you're not going to tell us where they are, Dr Maud?'

'How can I?' I replied, exasperated. 'How can I tell you something I don't know myself. By the way, thank you for returning the money. I did say I'd pay you a little more for your trouble, so why don't you take ten out of the cookie jar right away, then you'd better go.'

'Thanks,' Tony's partner said as helped himself to a ten pound note, but neither of them made a move to leave.

Tony looked at me sternly. 'OK Dr Maud, I'm going to give you one last chance to tell us where they are.'

'I've already explained, how can I tell you something I don't know myself?'

'I'm sorry but we'll have to do this the hard way. We're going to have to keep you here until you tell us.'

I forbore to point out that this was my home and I had no plans to go anywhere else right then.

'We're going to tie you up until you tell us. Would you sit in that chair please? Sit still while I find something to tie you with.'

This was getting farcical. I wondered if I was dreaming. He rummaged in my kitchen cupboards and discovered a first aid kit that I'd kept for years but never had any reason to use. He took out a few rolled bandages and a couple of triangular ones, all still in their original packages. He handed some to his partner and the two of them set about trying to bandage my legs to the chair legs. They were hopeless.

'I suppose you're 'Special Branch' too,' I said conversationally to the second youth.

'Special what?'

'Never mind,' I said gently, 'I know your friend is called Tony. What's your name?'

'I'm Jason,' he replied with a good-natured smile.

Tony was needing all his concentration as he struggled to tie a knot in the very short ends of the triangular bandage he used to tie my right leg to the chair, leaving me free to address my remarks directly to Jason.

'What are you both studying?' I asked him casually. I had of course recognised Tony's university student card earlier, when he flashed it at me claiming to be 'Special Branch'.

'Medicine,' he replied.

'What year?'

'First.'

'Are you enjoying it?'

'Oh yes, but it's more expensive that I thought it would be.'

'I suppose,' I probed carefully, 'someone's paying you to do this.'

'Yes,' he agreed readily. 'That's why we're here. We don't want to hurt you.'

'I know you don't want to hurt me, Jason,' I told him. 'You or Tony. But I have to warn you both, you could be in serious trouble for this. How much are you being paid?'

'Fifty each,' he replied. Tony nodded his agreement.

'Well, that's easily taken care of,' I said. 'I'll pay you seventy each if you untie me and tell me what this is all about.'

'A hundred each.'

'I took two hundred out of the cash machine yesterday. If I give you it all, that would leave me short of change, so how about seventy-five each?'

'Seventy-five each on top of the window cleaning money?'

'All right,' I sighed. I reckoned that if I could help straighten these two silly lads out it would be money well spent. 'Then when you've untied me I'll make us some sandwiches and you can tell me what's going on.'

Relief flooded their faces. 'You won't report us?'

'I don't want to ruin your careers if I don't have to, but I do need to know what's going on here. You'll find the ham in the fridge. Do you like mustard?'

As we sat at the kitchen table munching our sandwiches, their story unfolded. They had been in a pub the previous evening, short of cash as usual and making their beers last. They had got into conversation with a couple who came to sit near them. The man introduced himself and his girlfriend as Dave Smith and Peggy Browne. Dave asked them if they would be interested in earning some extra cash washing windows the next day.'

'What about your classes? Didn't you tell them you have lectures to attend?'

'Well, yeah, but Dave said the job wouldn't take long and we'd be finished and back for the afternoon. He met us early this morning to drive us here. He said he had arranged for his pal to drop off the equipment for us. We didn't know we had to go across on the ferry.'

'So did this Dave bring you across the ferry in his car this morning?'

'Yes, he dropped us on the main road at the

entrance to your street.'

'What colour was the car?'

'Black. Does it matter?'

I ignored the question. 'And was the window washing equipment waiting for you as promised?'

'Yes, we found the bucket and ladder and some cloths just outside your gate.'

'Did this Dave know you'd never washed windows before?' I asked.

Jason nodded. 'We told him that, but he said the window cleaning was just an excuse to look through your windows. He said he had agreed to collect a package from you addressed to Captain John Walker but he had to go to a meeting so he needed someone else to collect it for him. Dave said you might not be willing to give it to strangers so we should look to see which room it was in and then just pinch it. We were to call him as soon as we got it.'

'So that's why you used a ladder to reach the windows instead of a long squeegee. It was so you could get up and look through the windows into the house.'

They both nodded.

'Incidentally,' I was curious, 'what was supposed to happen after you called Dave Smith to tell him you'd found Captain Walker's package?'

'Dave said to call him as soon as we found it and meet him at the end of the road, where he dropped us off this morning. Actually, he called us himself at around ten to ask why we hadn't called him. We told him we'd looked into nearly all the rooms but hadn't seen any sign of it. He told us to keep looking.'

'All right,' I said, 'I understand all you've told me so far, and I can see now why you had the ladder at the window by the front door, Tony. You didn't need it to reach that window to wash it, did you? You needed to be up higher to see in properly.'

'That was the last window,' he said. 'I was about to call Dave and tell him we couldn't find any package when that Peggy Browne came along.'

'Yes,' Jason agreed heatedly. 'Called herself Mrs Walker! She wanted to get the package and letter herself. Probably wanted to do us out of getting paid.'

'I didn't want to hurt her,' said Tony. 'I didn't push the ladder, it started to slip and I didn't stop it because I thought it would miss her. I thought it would scare her though, you know, like make her realise we were there and could tell you that she wasn't Mrs Walker.'

I didn't quite believe him but I let it pass.

'Well,' I told them, 'I doubt that she'll be bringing a charge against you given the circumstances, but I have to tell you boys that I don't know this Captain John Walker. I haven't been keeping his mail for him, as Dave Smith suggested. The package arrived yesterday and a letter for him followed today. Both of them should have been on my hall table waiting to be returned but they've both disappeared. I can only think that someone has already taken them, I just can't think who or how. So why don't you call Dave Smith now and ask him to pick you up.'

'We called just before you got home but he said he couldn't come for us. He said he'd been called away and we should leave the window cleaning stuff here and make our own way back.'

'So you decided to have one more try to get the package by playing tough with me?'

They nodded, shamefacedly.

We sat in silence for a few minutes while we finished our sandwiches. Thinking through all they had told me, there was no longer any doubt in my mind that the man I had seen leaving the Bellevue Hotel in a hurry and whom I had followed to the ferry terminal was Dave Smith. The back of my neck felt tight.

'By the way,' I asked as casually as I could, 'what does Dave Smith look like?'

Jason replied cheerfully, 'Nothing special, just like a lot of other guys you meet in pubs. If I had to describe him, I'd say he's average height, dark wavy hair, a bit on the long side. He was wearing a nice leather jacket. A brown one. I wouldn't mind one like that myself.'

Bingo!

'Right,' I told my unlikely housebreakers, 'I've got things to do and it's time for you to go.' I took three fifties out of my purse. I doubted they'd ever see Dave Smith again, let alone get any money from him.

'Here's the money I promised you. I'm afraid you'll have to split one of the fifties between you. I've no more change. Off you go!'

'Could you possibly give us a ride to the ferry?' Jason asked.

I sighed. 'Alright, get in the car.'

6

Not surprisingly after that bizarre Tuesday I overslept Wednesday morning and was late getting dressed. In fact I had only just combed my hair and turned the bedclothes back to air when the doorbell rang. My bedside clock showed 8.25 am, which was a late start for me but was still early for callers. I peered through the side panel of the bay window in my bedroom which overlooks the front door. Standing at the door with their backs to me were two sturdy figures in black wearing police caps. I guessed they had come to question me about Peggy Browne's accident. I glanced in the mirror to check I was presentable then hurried to the door so as not to keep them waiting. I hoped Peggy Browne's head injury had not turned out to be worse than first appeared. I unlocked the door and opened it to invite the two policemen in, prepared to explain how the accident had occurred and how I had taken Peggy to A&E.

The next thing I knew, my next door neighbour, Richard Carter, was bending over me saying, 'Angelina, are you all right? Angelina, wake up! What happened? Did you fall?'

‘I must have been asleep.’ I replied blearily. I opened my eyes and looked around. My head started to pound with the movement. Everything was blurred at first but as my focus improved I could see that I was lying on my side on the tiled floor of my hallway. The door was wide open and I was freezing cold. My head hurt when I moved it. I couldn’t understand what I was doing on the floor of my hallway. I had no recollection of how I got there. And why was the front door wide open letting in all that cold air? Why was Richard Carter there? I had to get up and find out what was happening. Keeping my head as still as I could because it hurt so much to move it, I slowly eased myself up to a sitting position against the wall. The walls spun gently round.

‘Angelina, please don’t try to get up too quickly,’ Richard was saying anxiously. ‘You may have broken a hip. You can break a hip falling you know.’

I was leaning on the door jamb with my legs stretched out in front of me. I tentatively pulled up first one, then the other. It didn’t hurt to move either leg. I then tried raising each arm in turn and they didn’t hurt either. That was fine, but while I was glad to find my legs and arms were intact, it felt very uncomfortable sitting down there on the hard floor. I needed to get up. I tried to pull myself up but was too dizzy.

‘Just stay there, Angelina. Don’t try to get up. I’m calling for help right now.’

What a bossy neighbour!

'I'm not staying down here, Richard,' I told him. 'It's too hard and too cold.'

'I think you should.'

'Well I'm not going to.' I began to lever myself to a kneeling position.

'All right, let me help you if you're going to insist on getting up. I don't think you should though.'

With Richard's help I pulled myself unsteadily to my feet. The hallway spun again, much faster this time than when I was down on the floor. Fortunately he is tall, and by half leaning on him and half clinging to him I managed to stay upright. When the spinning stopped he helped me stagger slowly from the freezing hallway into the kitchen. I think he muttered something about wilful women and this not being a good idea but I didn't care, I was just grateful to be lowered into a comfortable chair. I felt weak and my eyes didn't want to focus. Why was it all such an effort?

After a while my head cleared a little. I leaned gratefully against the padded chair back and gazed around my familiar kitchen, taking care to move my head as little as possible. It was my kitchen all right but it was horribly wrong. The room was all higgledy-piggledy. Was I hallucinating or in the middle of a bad dream? The cupboard doors were all wide open and lots of things which should have been in them were on the floor. There was flour scattered and sugar and baking things strewn around, and all my china was stacked any old how on the counter. The fridge door was wide open and the oven doors too. The floor by the fridge looked wet as though something had been spilled on it.

Maybe I really was dreaming. Maybe if I closed my eyes and then opened them again everything would be back to normal. My head was so painful that I kept my eyes closed for a minute or two. When I did open them again I became aware of the large red numerals of the digital clock on the microwave straight ahead of me. They read 10.56 am. And the microwave door was open too.

As I sat there numbly I became aware of voices which seemed to be coming nearer.

'The door's open.'

'Angelina must have left it open for us.'

'She doesn't usually.'

'Shall we just go in then?'

In a moment of clarity my mind connected the clock and the voices. It must be Wednesday. It was my turn to host our monthly neighbourhood coffee morning, fourth Wednesday in the month. What was I going to do? I couldn't even get up from the chair.

Then I heard Richard's voice coming from the hallway.

'Had a fall ... yes, I've called an ambulance ... sorry about this ... yes, they told me it's coming right away ... no, I think we're all right ... yes, I'll let you know ... '

Then Richard, bless him, was by my side again.

'Don't worry,' he said gently. 'Everything's taken care of. The ambulance is on its way. You've had an accident and you've been unconscious. Your door was wide open this morning when I came over for coffee and I found you lying there on the floor. '

He paused, giving me time to digest this information.

'Angelina,' he probed gently, 'do you remember slipping or losing your balance?'

'No.'

'You see, there's something worrying me. Why was your door open? I've just been and examined it carefully and can't find any signs that it was forced. Also your door is unlocked, which means that unless you forgot to lock it last night you must have opened it this morning for some reason. Can you remember if anyone came to the door?'

'Only the policemen.'

'What policemen?'

'The doorbell. They rang the doorbell.'

'When was this?'

Here was a question I could answer because I had seen the time on the bedroom clock.

'Twenty five past eight.'

Richard was quiet then and I was glad of it because I didn't feel well at all and it hurt my head to think. I must have lost consciousness again because the next thing I remember was waking up in a hospital bed wearing a white plastic wrist band and a floral nightie.

7

'Do you feel ready to sit up for some breakfast?' The nurse was a pleasant-faced, middle-aged woman. She set a tray on the mobile table beside my bed.

'I'm going to raise you up slowly,' she said, 'and I want you to tell me straight away if it makes you feel dizzy.'

She pressed the button to raise the top end of my bed and lever me into a sitting position. It was surprisingly comfortable.

'Is that all right? Do you feel dizzy at all?'

'Actually, I feel just fine,' I told her. 'But what am I doing here? I can see that I'm in a hospital but how did I get here?'

'I don't know what happened,' she said, easing my pillows. 'You must have been in some kind of accident. You came in yesterday from A&E with a head injury. It must have been quite a bang because you were unconscious when you came in. How does it feel now?'

I put my hand up to my head. I could feel a lump on the left side. It felt sore if I pressed it but there was no pain otherwise. I moved my head cautiously from side to side. There was no pain or dizziness. Next I tried moving my chin gently to my chest and experienced no problem there either. I tried rotating my head slowly. Rotation, like the other head movements caused no discomfort. So far so good. I moved a finger slowly from side to side in front of my eyes and then up and down. I could see my finger clearly wherever I held it. When I drew it towards my nose I could still see it clearly. No damage there.

This was all very encouraging. I covered one ear.

'Say something please,' I said to the nurse.

'What?' she responded to my unexpected request.

'Fine,' I said, covering the other ear. 'What's for breakfast?'

'Porridge,' she replied, staring at me. 'And juice and toast and marmalade if you want it.'

Both ears were functioning.

'Thanks,' I said happily. 'I'd love some breakfast.'

I must have been hungry. I sprinkled a little salt on the porridge, added a generous dollop of milk from the small bottle I found on my tray and ate it with relish. Then I spread butter and marmalade on the two slices of toast provided and wolfed those too. The cup of tea that came on a separate trolley rounded the meal off nicely.

I was in one of four beds in a large pleasant room. From my bed I could see that the large window looked out over water in the distance. My three companions were all hooked up to drips. Two of them were not given breakfast in accordance with the printed notices posted above their beds. The third was picking at her food. She looked very poorly.

By contrast I was feeling fit and rested. I felt I had no excuse to be taking up a hospital bed that someone else might need. I told the nurse so when she came to collect my breakfast tray.

'Where did you put my clothes?' I asked her. 'I think I'll get dressed. There's no need for me to stay here any longer.'

'Dr Maud, I think you'd better stay put until the doctor's been and had a word with you. You can call your husband when the doctor says you can go home.'

'My husband?'

'You won't remember of course because you were unconscious at the time, but when your husband brought you in yesterday he asked us to give him a call when you're ready to go home. By the way, he's quite a dish, isn't he?'

Fine I thought, except for the fact that I don't have a husband. On the other hand perhaps I did have a husband and the blow on my head had caused me to forget. After all, I didn't remember coming to the hospital. And if I did have a husband, would I recognise him when he came to collect me? What if a complete stranger was pretending to be my husband? How would I know if he was my husband or a stranger? Well, all I could do was to wait and see. A dish? Interesting.

'All right,' I said to the nurse, 'I'll wait.'

I didn't have to wait long before a different nurse looked into the room and announced, 'Someone here to see you, Dr Maud.'

Goodness, I didn't have as much as a comb to tidy myself up. I quickly ran my fingers through my hair. That would have to do for the doctor or perhaps the dishy husband I didn't remember. However, the visitor the nurse ushered in was neither the doctor nor the unknown husband. It was a tall, athletic-looking young man. As soon as I saw the police cap he was carrying I recoiled involuntarily.

'It's all right, Dr Maud, don't be frightened.' The nurse took my hand. 'You look as if you saw a ghost. This is PC Hamilton. He wants to talk to you. Would you like me to stay with you?'

I gripped her hand tightly. 'Yes, please.'

'Good morning, Dr Maud,' he introduced himself, 'I'm PC Hamilton. I hope you're feeling up to talking to me this morning. I just want to ask you a few questions about the break-in at your house yesterday. If you're not up to it yet I can come back later.'

An image of my kitchen in chaos and the clock on my microwave began to come back to me now that my memory had been jogged by the mention of the break-in. I also recognised the policeman. I didn't know him personally, but knew his mother. I relaxed a little and tried not to sound flustered. 'I'm sorry, I didn't recognise you at first. I know who you are, your mother's in my spinning group. She's spinning wool right now to make ...' Just in time I stopped myself from informing this young man that his mother was spinning wool to knit him a Fair Isle sweater for Christmas.

'That's all right, Dr Maud, I know about the sweater.' He grinned. 'You've lived in Dunoon long enough to know it's impossible to keep a secret here.'

There was some truth in what he said. Our thirteen mile stretch of coastal community is interwoven throughout by a grapevine of family connections, school associations and common interest groups. It is said locally that if you sneeze at the north end, someone will immediately say 'bless you' at the south end, and vice versa.

'The reason I'm here is to follow up on a report of a break in at your house yesterday, during which you were knocked unconscious. Can you tell me anything about it?'

'Very little, I'm afraid. I just have a vague recollection of a mess in my kitchen and I remember seeing 10.56 on the red digital clock on the microwave.'

'We've been up to your house and it looks like all the rooms have been thoroughly searched. We think that whoever broke in was looking for something. Have you any idea what they were after? Any valuables, jewels, art work, antiques or anything in the house that someone might want to get their hands on?'

'I really don't have any idea,' I told him. 'I've never had much interest in jewellery or art work and I keep very little money in the house now that we use plastic for everything. My laptop computer is probably the only thing worth taking and that sits in full view on my desk. I suppose my car would be worth taking too, but that would be in the garage, not the house. I can have a look round when I get home and let you know if anything's missing. They might have been looking for something but right now I can't think what it could be.'

It was only after PC Hamilton had left that I recalled the package and letter addressed to Captain John Walker.

8

Later that morning the nurse brought in a second visitor.

'Your husband's come to see you. So now that the doctor has been and said you're OK, he can take you home.'

I saw the look of surprise on my neighbour's face, but he rose to the occasion and thanked the nurse politely. He waited until she disappeared, then grinned and gallantly assured me that he was honoured to be taken for the husband of so great a lady. He was delighted when I told him that he was considered a 'dish' by the hospital staff. We left the hospital ward in good spirits with happy smiles and thanks to all.

Once out of the hospital building, Richard's easygoing manner altered. He looked carefully round the car park then took my arm, marched me to quickly to his parked car, hustled me into the seat and slammed the door. He moved quickly to the driver's side and scanned the car park once again before getting into the car himself. I wondered why he was rushing me like that. Why hadn't he suggested I wait inside while he drove his car up to the door? Did he not want to be seen with me? Had he got a jealous wife or girlfriend? I had never seen a woman next door, but that didn't necessarily mean he didn't have one around somewhere. Maybe he was just sick of pretending the 'husband' charade was fun and had more important things to do than drive me home.

Whatever his reasons, I was grateful to him for getting me to the hospital in the first place and then for coming to take me home. I would just thank him for all his trouble and maybe ask him over for dinner soon.

He didn't say anything more as we buckled our seat belts, and remained silent as he drove down to the shore road, then parked along a quiet stretch.

Eventually, he said, 'Tell me, Angelina, is there someone, maybe a relative, you could go and stay with for a couple of weeks?'

Grateful as I was for all his help, I considered that where I chose to stay was really none of his business. In fact his question was bordering on interference. The hospital doctor had pronounced me fit to go home and I was perfectly capable of taking care of myself in my own house. I knew from the police visit that morning that it was in a bit of a mess, but I could easily sort that out.

'Well, I suppose so,' I responded doubtfully, not wishing to offend him. 'But Richard, I really don't need to go anywhere. I'm fully recovered and don't need anyone to look after me. I was told by the policeman who came to see me this morning that my house is a mess so I'm prepared for that. I can take care of it. I'm not ill. Honestly, I don't need to go away and recuperate.'

He was silent again for a moment. Then he said carefully, 'I'm guessing you don't remember much of what happened yesterday?'

'Not really. As I told PC Hamilton this morning, I remember sitting in a chair in the kitchen and everything seemed to be in an awful mess. I think things were out of the cupboards and on the floor. I do definitely remember the red digital clock on the microwave though, saying 10.56, but that's about all. The policeman mentioned that other rooms in the house had been disturbed too, but I'm not worried. I can soon clear it all up.'

He looked at me thoughtfully. 'Angelina, just before you lost consciousness in the kitchen yesterday, you said something to me about two policemen coming to your house. You even knew the time they came. What did the police officer that came to the hospital have to say about them?'

'Oh no!' I gasped. 'Can you believe it? I forgot to mention them to PC Hamilton! I must have been still a bit shocked by the sight of his cap when he arrived. He just asked me about what thieves might have been looking for, jewellery and such, and I was busy explaining that I don't have anything in the house that would be worth breaking in for other than the TV and my computer and

I clean forgot to tell him about those two policemen. In fact I forgot about the package and letter too until after he'd gone so I didn't tell him about those either.'

'A package and a letter? How do they fit into the picture? Were you mailing something valuable? Is that what the thieves were looking for?'

'No,' I explained, 'the package and letter were sent to me. Actually they weren't sent to me exactly, they were sent to a Captain John Walker at my address. Yes, now I think about it, I'm sure that must have been what the thieves must have been after.'

Richard was clearly puzzled.

'Well, what was inside the package and what did the letter say? Who sent them?'

'I've no idea. Why would I open them? They weren't addressed to me, and there was no return address. I arranged to return the package to the carrier and was planning to take the letter to the post box, but they both disappeared.'

'They couldn't disappear for no reason. Why would you think the thieves were after misdirected mail?'

'Because,' I tried not to sound irritated by his questioning, ' because first I had a phone call from a man about them and then some medical students pretending to be window cleaners came looking for them. Then a woman claiming to be Captain John Walker's wife came to the door asking for them and then there was the accident with the window cleaner's ladder. Actually, when those two policemen came to the house yesterday morning, I thought it was to ask me about the accident with the ladder.'

'Angelina, I'm getting confused. How were you hit on the head by a ladder and who called the police? There was no one with you when I found you. I came over to your house for coffee and there you were, lying unconscious in the doorway.'

'No, Richard,' I started to explain, 'I wasn't hit by the ladder. It was a woman called Peggy Browne.'

Richard started the car engine.

'I think, Angelina, I'd better get you back to the hospital so they can keep an eye on you. It sounds as though you're still pretty concussed. You shouldn't be travelling anywhere until you're thinking clearly.'

'Please Richard, just stop and let me explain.'

He looked doubtful.

I said, 'Let me start at the beginning. The whole thing began on Monday. That was when the package for Captain John Walker arrived. It was on Tuesday that the letter followed. A short time after the letter arrived on Tuesday a man phoned about the package. Shortly after the phone call two bogus window cleaners came and it turned out that they were also looking for the package. While they were still cleaning my windows a woman claiming to be Mrs Walker, wife of Captain John Walker, arrived and said she'd come to collect his package. None of them asked about the letter but I did tell Peggy Browne about it because I believed she was Mrs Walker at the time. I explained that I couldn't give her either the package or the letter because they had both disappeared. Then she was accidentally hit on the head when the window cleaner's ladder fell and I took her to A&E. That's where I discovered she was Peggy Browne, not Mrs. Walker.'

'Peggy Browne was hit on the head?' Richard looked startled. ' You also mentioned a phone call. Did the man say who he was?'

'No, he rang off when I asked him.'

'Angelina, we're looking at a more than a simple break-in here. Tell me more about those two policemen that came to your house yesterday morning. You told me when I found you yesterday that you noted the time they came.'

'Yes, I know exactly when it was. It was 8.25 yesterday morning.'

Richard listened carefully as I recalled how I had been in my bedroom when the doorbell rang, and saw the two police caps through the bedroom window.

'Did they show you any ID when they came to the door?'

'No. You see, when I saw the police caps I assumed they had come to question me about Peggy Browne's accident. I just rushed to answer the door.'

'And you remember nothing after that?'

'No.'

'Until you found yourself in the middle of a mess in the kitchen and saw 10.56 on the microwave clock. Do you remember anything else?'

'Well, I think I was very cold. I think I was lying on the floor with the front door open.'

'Yes, you were. That's where I found you.'

'I really am grateful to you, Richard. Thank you so much for everything.' He shrugged, 'Glad to be of help. But seriously, Angelina, I need to be sure I have the complete picture. You've told me snippets of what's been happening, but if you feel up to it, I'd like to go over the whole thing again and try to make sense of it. I want to be sure you're out of danger.'

I wasn't really sure that it was my neighbour's business, but the idea of being in danger was rather startling and he had certainly been very kind so I told him the whole story again from the beginning.

When I'd finished, Richard said, 'Peggy Browne. I seem to have heard that name before. Did you overhear anything else about her while you were at A&E?'

'Only that she was supposed to meet her boyfriend, Dave Smith, back at the Bellevue Hotel. They had stayed there overnight.'

That got his attention.

'Dave Smith. Are you quite sure?'

'Yes.'

Richard started the car. As we drove along he told me that my whole house had been thoroughly turned over during the time I had lain unconscious in my hallway.

'You must realise, Angelina, that this was not a casual break-in,' he said. 'And those men you took to be police would have been looking for the letter and package too. Did you search for them yourself when you got home after taking Peggy Browne to the hospital on Tuesday?'

'Of course I did,' I told him. 'Even though I remembered quite clearly putting both the package and the letter on the hall table when they arrived.'

'Do you think it's possible that the window cleaners took them?' Richard speculated.

'Oh no, definitely not,' I assured him. 'They were still searching for them when I got back from taking Peggy to the hospital.'

'So,' Richard mused, 'all Tuesday's attempts to collect the package from you failed because somehow both the package and the letter that followed it had mysteriously disappeared shortly after arrival. That's obviously why those two thugs were sent to your house yesterday to find them. Someone wants them very badly and assumes you still have them.'

Richard turned into my driveway.

'Stay in the car,' he told me, 'while I check the house is empty.'

Going over the events of the week with

Richard had unnerved me and I was glad to comply. There was nothing to suggest there were intruders in my house, such as a strange car in the driveway or out on the street, but I was still glad he was checking before I went in.

'Just a minute though,' I called to him as he got out of the car, 'I don't have my handbag with me, so I don't have a key to get in.'

Richard waved a key at me. 'I came prepared,' he said. 'I brought your spare key with me.'

The previous year, Richard and I had exchanged spare keys as neighbours often do for emergency access, or in the event of a key being lost. I thought this a wise precaution at the time but had never really expected it to be necessary.

Richard let himself into the house and emerged a few minutes later, announcing,

'All clear!' Then he added, 'But be prepared for a shock when you see the state of the house when you go in. Would you like me to come with you?'

'Well,' I replied, 'the first thing I'm going to do is make a cup of tea. Would you like one?'

He followed me into the house.

9

I was expecting a mess in my kitchen but was not prepared for the degree of devastation that met me. The kitchen looked as though it had been attacked. Cupboard doors were not just open, some of the hinges had been wrenched and a couple of doors hung crazily. Flour bags and dry cereal packets had been emptied out on the counters, the contents spilling over onto the floor. Coffee grounds and broken biscuits crunched underfoot. My cookie jar, in which I keep loose change, lay on its side broken. There were a few bank notes and coins amid the debris on the floor. Mugs and china were everywhere, hopefully none broken. Drawers had been pulled out completely, emptied out and thrown on the floor with their contents. Cleaning fluids which had spilled out of bottles lying on their sides made pools on the floor.

'You'd better look at the rest of the house,' Richard said.

I did. My house has a kitchen/dining area, a living room, three bedrooms, one *en suite*, a second one ready for guests and a small third one that I use as an office, with a fold-up futon for additional guest use. There is a separate guest bathroom. Richard stayed in the kitchen while I went systematically through each room. Each one had suffered the same treatment as the kitchen. Some of the living room furniture had been overturned, some pushed aside. The contents of my needlework cabinet lay in a heap on the floor. The table was covered with open books and torn magazines. The piano was open and sheet music from the piano stool box scattered on the floor.

In the bedrooms, furniture was pulled away from the walls, beds were stripped, mattresses removed and slit open. Cupboards were open, clothes thrown around the rooms and drawers emptied and left on the floor with their contents. In the bathroom, the bath was pulled away from the wall and stood at an angle. The medicine cabinet was open and empty. I trod on a toothpaste tube and almost slipped on the extruded contents camouflaged by towels on the floor. The corridor outside the bedrooms was strewn with sheets and towels from the airing cupboard.

My office was just a mass of scattered paper. The bookshelves were empty, the books thrown on the floor. Carefully filed documents, statements and receipts were jumbled up with sheets of unused computer paper from two previously unopened packages. Curiously, my computer and printer appeared to have been untouched.

I went back into the kitchen. Richard was still there.

'I'll tell you what Angelina,' he said, 'leave all this for now and come over to my place and I'll make you a good strong cup of coffee. You look as though you need it.'

I followed him meekly. Right then, the wanton devastation of my home and the prospect of clearing it all up was too much.

10

I rang my sister Gabriella from Richard's house. He was right in advising me to stay elsewhere while the police conducted their investigation and until they apprehended the perpetrators of the break in. Occurrences of this kind are far from normal in our quiet neighbourhood, populated largely by retirees like myself. I finally conceded that it might be dangerous for me to stay here if those thugs were still looking for the missing package and letter. As Richard reminded me, I had already been knocked unconscious once and ended up overnight in hospital. I surely didn't want to risk a repeat visit. He also pointed out that there was no hurry to clean up the mess in my house. It would still be there waiting for me when I returned. He was right of course. As I dialled my sister's number it also occurred to me that I might persuade Gabriella to come back with me to help clear the mess up.

My sister Gabriella and I are identical twins, I being the elder by twenty minutes. This is something she needs reminding of from time to time. As children, our parents dressed us alike, and like many other twins we still enjoy identity confusion. We went on to medical school together and only separated when our career paths took us in different directions, mine to general practice and Gabriella's to psychiatry. We both married and had families. I have two sons and a daughter, all now living and working in the United States. Gabriella has one son, George, who is a civil servant in London. I've never been able to pin down exactly what George does, other than his work takes him abroad sometimes.

Gabriella and I are both widowed. On retirement after practicing in Glasgow I moved to the scenic west coast of Scotland. Gabriella stayed in East Anglia after working for many years near Norwich. Since retiring, she has tried her hand in one art pursuit after another. The cookie jar in my kitchen, from which I extracted cash for the 'window cleaners' two days ago, was a product of her pottery phase.

We have never needed a reason to visit each other, so I didn't bother to explain the reason for this particular visit over the phone. That could keep until I arrived.

She was delighted. Her only question was whether I had changed my telephone number because she didn't recognise the number on her caller ID.

'No, my number's still the same,' I assured her. 'I'm calling from a friend's house.'

That was another explanation that could

wait until I arrived.

I told Gabriella that there was nothing to wait for, so I would set off to drive south that afternoon. I would stop overnight in York, then continue on to her home in Bungay the following morning.

'If I set off early from York tomorrow,' I told her, 'I should be with you in time for lunch. I'll stay for a couple of weeks if that's OK.'

Arrangements with Gabriella completed, I thanked Richard for all his kindness, assured him once again that I was now able to manage on my own and felt strong enough to drive to Gabriella's. I returned to my own house to collect clothes, toiletries and other necessities for a couple of weeks away from home. The first thing I needed to find was my handbag. That turned out to be easy. The bag lay open and empty on the floor near the window in my study. Finding its contents, however, might be more difficult. Like the contents of my clothes drawers, the handbag's contents had been tipped out and were strewn around the floor. I picked up my mobile phone and checked it. The battery was low but it still worked; I could charge it up later. I searched without much hope for my purse, and to my surprise and delight discovered it under a heap of scarves and lingerie. To my even further surprise and delight, my credit cards, debit cards and cash were still in their proper slots. My spare car key was still in one of the purse's little compartments. That was certainly one less complication to deal with.

However, the fact that nothing had been taken from my purse or from my jewellery case, or even cash from the cookie jar, was confirmation that the bogus policemen were not run of the mill burglars. They had been looking only for the missing package and letter. I rang Richard from my mobile to tell him this. I also told him that since I had found my purse, contents intact, so long as my car was not damaged, I would set off straight away for the first leg of my drive to Bungay. His response rather surprised me. Instead of suggesting I allow time to recover before undertaking a long drive south as I expected, he urged me to set off as quickly as possible, not to linger in the house a moment longer than necessary while the intruders were still at large.

I picked out what was needed for the visit from the items strewn around the bedroom and bathroom as quickly as I could and packed them into an overnight bag. I didn't need to take a lot because I can always borrow clothes from Gabriella, the two of us being the same size. Leaving the house as I found it I hefted my handbag over my shoulder, picked up my overnight bag and locked the front door.

By this time I was not surprised to find the garage in a similar state to the rest of the house. Gardening tools were pulled off their wall hangers and thrown on the floor. Shelf contents, weed killer, garden gloves, and assorted tools, plant pots, packets of seeds etc., were likewise strewn over the floor. My car hadn't escaped. The boot was open and the flat boxes I keep in the boot to prevent shopping bags spilling had been ripped up. A tartan travelling rug was on the floor of the garage along with emptied potting soil and lawn fertilizer sacks. Inside the car, the glove compartment and door pocket contents were scattered over the front seats and the floor. I picked up enough to clear the driving seat and stuffed it back as best I could.

Despite the havoc that surrounded me, there appeared to be no actual damage to the car itself, so I shut the doors, threw my overnight bag into the boot, got in and tried the engine. It started. At least the battery had not run down and the car was still working. I backed out, locked the garage door and was finally ready to go. The clean-up operation could wait until I got home again. I turned the car round and set off up my driveway. Richard was waiting for me at the gate. He handed me a package.

'Ham sandwiches and a bottle of water for your journey,' he said. 'Don't bother getting out of the car to close the gate. I'll do it. Safe journey!'

I hadn't realised until then that I was hungry and I certainly wouldn't have thought to close the gate as I left. As the nurse at the hospital said earlier that morning, Richard Carter really was a dish.

11

Leaving Dunoon, the sun was shining and the sea was calm. Along the coast road towards the terminal at Hunters Quay, I could see the red and white ferry coming to take me over to the mainland. Leaving the mayhem in my house behind, I was able to view the situation objectively. The police would take care of those responsible for the break in and my homeowner's policy would take care of the damage. Richard had promised to monitor progress and keep me informed. There was nothing to be gained by dwelling on what I was leaving behind. I thought of his kindness as I munched the ham sandwiches he had prepared for me during the ferry crossing. Bless him, he had even included a small packet of shortbread biscuits. Much later, it dawned on me that he must have given me his own lunch!

I drove off the ferry at McInroy's point and followed the road through the old towns of Gourock, Greenock and Port Glasgow, past the remnants of the giant shipbuilding industry along the banks of the river Clyde. Large imposing stone houses along the road testified to past prosperity. These houses once looked down over one of the most important and prosperous shipbuilding areas in the world.

The scenery along the south bank of the River Clyde changed after Port Glasgow from urban to pastoral, the old towns giving way to green fields and grazing sheep. Driving then along the M8, the east-west arterial that takes one through Glasgow and on to Edinburgh, the capital of Scotland, I passed the airport on my left. I saw a few tails of aeroplanes parked at arrival/ departure gates although I couldn't tell at that distance which airlines they belonged to. They could have been United or Iceland Air which are our direct transatlantic carriers, or Emirates flying east. They could also have been the less exotic but equally important domestic carriers or charter planes.

On the outskirts of Glasgow, I exited onto the M74 which took me to the M6 south. Traffic was not heavy that day and the weather was fine so I made good time passing through the rural countryside of southern Scotland.

I crossed the border from Scotland to England no longer worried about the situation I had left behind. On the contrary I was glad to get away from it. Richard Carter had been right to suggest I go away for a couple of weeks. His idea that I might still be in danger was surely over the top, but I was certainly grateful to him for finding me unconscious yesterday and getting me to the hospital, not to mention bringing me home again today, and providing sandwiches for the journey.

I was looking forward to being with Gabriella again too. She is fun to be with, always involved in some interesting project or other. Furthermore, I knew she would be more than willing to come back to Scotland with me in a couple of weeks' time to help put my house to rights.

I drove on past fields, sheep and dry stone walls. The A66 took me across the Pennines to the A1 south on the way to York. We no longer have family there to visit, but there is a particular hotel by the river with a good restaurant that Gabriella and I have both used as a stop-off point for several years.

I was thinking about this as I passed into Yorkshire, which led me to thinking how we are creatures of habit, sitting on the same seats in church, the same seats in a meeting and how I invariably drink coffee mid-morning and tea mid-afternoon. Along with my musings came the realisation that it was in fact mid-afternoon and it was time to stop for a tea break. It also occurred to me that my mind should have been on my driving, not wandering off at tangents. It was definitely time for a tea break. I decided to pull in at the first pub I came to when I branched off the A1.

With my attention now back on the road, I became aware that another vehicle, a light-coloured SUV, was close behind me on the turnoff. For some reason the back of my neck began to prickle. I figured my imagination must be going haywire, probably the result of Richard's unnecessary forebodings combined with the need for a cup of tea. Well, I could easily take care of that. I drove more slowly to allow the other vehicle to pass. But it didn't pass; it stayed behind me. I increased my speed. The SUV followed, keeping the same distance between us. I tried again, this time slowing almost to a crawl and keeping well to the side of the road. I was not overtaken. Maybe I had a nervous driver behind me who didn't care to overtake. I increased my speed again, leaving the SUV way behind me. As I rounded a bend I spotted a pub ahead on the left hand side of the road. Perfect! I pulled off the road smartly in front of the pub and watched carefully as the SUV drove by. It was a light-tan vehicle. It looked fairly new, but was otherwise unremarkable. I guessed from his silhouette that the driver was a man, though I couldn't see him properly. I could see the passenger much more clearly; he was definitely male. They drove on past without so much as a glance in my direction. Indeed, the passenger was turned towards the driver and seemed to be talking heatedly to him if his gesticulations were anything to go by.

Relieved, I locked my blue Beetle and went into the pub for that much needed cup of tea. Once inside though, I found a seat by a window looking out onto the road so that I could watch to see if the tan SUV came back. Just in case.

I nursed my cup up tea for a good ten minutes, all the time watching through the window. The SUV did not return and I felt I must have been rather paranoid imagining it could be anything to do with me. It was time to get on the road again. The SUV would already be several miles nearer to its destination while I was sipping tea in the pub.

The rest of the drive to York was uneventful but, paranoid or not, I was glad of the reassuring sight of the Minster towers as I approached. My hotel by the river had become a familiar home from home over the years too. I turned into the car park and, just to be on the safe side, drove round the other parked vehicles to check whether there was a tan SUV among them. Having reassured myself that it was not there, I selected my own parking spot, well out of sight of the road.

In the rush to leave my house right away at Richard's urging, I had completely forgotten to call ahead to book a room in the hotel. If there was no vacancy I would have to find another hotel. There was no point in carrying my overnight bag into the hotel with me until I knew whether or not I had a room, so I left it in the car boot. Grabbing just my shoulder bag containing my purse and a light jacket, I hurried to the reception desk. It turned out that the hotel not only had a vacancy, they were able to give me a room overlooking the river.

The usual tray with the means of making

tea or instant coffee, together with a couple of biscuits was a welcome sight. I made coffee and took it to the little table by the window. There were lots of people down below on the riverside walk enjoying the sunshine. It was far too nice to stay indoors and I needed to stretch my legs after sitting in the car for so long so I decided to go for a walk along the river bank myself. I finished the coffee and biscuits, slipped on my jacket, removed several heavy items, water bottle, toiletries etc. from my shoulder bag to make it lighter, and headed out.

The River Ouse flows serenely through York. At one time, river barges would deliver goods to large warehouses along the river bank. Since those days, the riverside has become more gentrified with pleasant walks and seats for people to sit and enjoy the scenery and watch the boats on the river. A sight-seeing boat full of tourists chugged past me. Some children were waving from the boat to the people along the river bank. I waved back. A few smaller pleasure boats passed by too but they paid no attention to we landlubbers. Further along the river walk a cluster of people were watching something. I went to see what was happening. A small group of art students were sitting on the river bank with sketching pads balanced on their knees sketching the scene before them. It was interesting to see each artist's interpretation of the river scene and the different aspects each one had chosen to focus on. I stayed quite a while watching and admiring their work.

I left the river walk at Lendal Bridge to revisit a few familiar city landmarks. The museum gardens were on my left. Did peacocks still roam the gardens as they did in my childhood and did the natural history museum still have a dinosaur exhibit? The public library, next to the museum gardens, was a popular haunt during my schooldays. I peeked inside to see if much had changed. Gratifyingly little had changed beyond furniture realignment. My walk took me past the beautiful York Minster, built on the site of a Roman fortress. I went into the Minster through the Great West Door and walked slowly round, drawn into the sense of reverence which pervades this magnificent cathedral. Emerging from it, I continued on through Petergate and into the narrow Shambles, where upstairs windows overhang the narrow street below. The Shambles was once a street of butchers' shops. Nowadays it is one of York's tourist magnets, and it is to the tourist market that the little shops now cater.

The afternoon was merging into early evening by the time I wandered back to the hotel. It had been quite a while since I'd enjoyed Richard's ham sandwiches on the ferry crossing and I was definitely peckish. I still had to collect my overnight bag from my car but decided that could wait until I'd checked the hotel dinner menu out. The hotel had a restaurant which led off from the foyer so that would be my first choice if the menu looked promising.

A group of people was slowly progressing through the hotel entrance. From the scraps of conversation I overheard as I followed them in, they had enjoyed dining there before and were looking forward to doing so again. Peeking through the door into the restaurant I could see that the tables were rapidly filling up. It was obvious that the restaurant was very popular so I immediately joined the short queue of people waiting for tables while they were still available. The overnight bag could be collected from the car later.

One of the menu items was liver and onions. I looked no further down the list and was soon tucking in to one of my favourite dishes served with mashed potatoes and grilled tomatoes, all nicely garnished with watercress. There is nothing like comfort food at the end of a long day. Liver and onions had never tasted so good. When the waitress later offered to bring the dessert trolley I nodded eagerly and watched with anticipation as she wheeled it towards me.

Behind the dessert trolley, two men were being shown to the recently vacated table next to mine. I noticed them in my peripheral vision but had no reason to pay any attention to them until suddenly the shorter of the two fixed his gaze on me and gave a start. He turned and whispered something to his companion, whereupon both men turned abruptly and walked back out of the restaurant, leaving their waiter staring after them. The waiter must have seen the surprise on my face too.

'Is everything all right, madam?' he asked.

'Oh yes, I'm fine,' I assured him. After all, common sense said the incident was nothing to do with me. I had never seen either of the two men before. Nevertheless I had to admit to myself that I was a little shaken by the incident. I no longer had any appetite for the delights of the dessert trolley. Deflated, I just asked for the bill.

Leaving the restaurant I felt more and more uneasy about the way those two men had turned and left so abruptly. One of them certainly seemed to recognise me even though I didn't recognise either of them. I looked nervously round the hotel foyer as I left, to see if they were still there. There was no sign of them inside the hotel, but I still had to go outside to the car park to retrieve my overnight bag in the car boot.

It was still light enough outside to see clearly. I went out to the car park and paused at the entry, glancing round carefully to see if the two mystery men were there before going to my car. Again there was no sign of them. The car park had really filled up though since I arrived. Remembering the tan SUV that sat behind me on the way to York, I scanned the other vehicles for one that might be a match. There were several SUVs parked, as one might expect, but none were light coloured. Somewhat reassured, I walked quickly over to the Beetle, opened the bonnet and collected my overnight bag. I locked the car up for the night and after a final glance around the car park for the two men, hurried back to the safety of the hotel and up to my room on the third floor.

It took a minute or two to take in what had happened to my room since leaving it just a few hours ago to go out for a walk. The scene was reminiscent of my house back in Scotland. I was horrified. The bed had been stripped and bedclothes left in a heap on the floor. The mattress lay lopsidedly across one corner of the foot of the bed. The doors to the empty wardrobe swung open exposing empty hangers. Drawers, likewise empty, were piled on the bed springs. A folded ironing board lay on the floor together with the television set which had been pulled out from its slot next to the dresser, leaving wires dangling from the wall. I went into the bathroom. Towels had been removed from their rack and thrown in the bath, together with soap and shampoo. I went back into the main room. The table by the window, where I had looked out on the river scene earlier, was still in place but its little drawer was pulled right out. The welcome tray was on the floor. The items I had put in the top dresser drawer were on the floor. This was not burglary, the room had been thoroughly searched. I picked up the telephone and put the receiver to my ear. At least, amid the mayhem, that was still working. I called the front desk to report the situation.

The hotel manager responded to my call right away. She came straight to my room, together with a hotel security guard. If she was shocked by the scene that met her she didn't show it. In fact both she and the security guard appeared perfectly calm. She apologised profusely for the inconvenience, expressing great concern that this should have happened to a guest. In fact, she seemed less worried about the state of the room than the distress it might have caused me. She assured me that I would be given a different room for the night, an upgrade, and that the charge would be waived. I was absorbing this turn of events when she picked up my overnight bag and firmly ushered me out of the room. I suggested we should call the police but the manager assured me that it wouldn't be necessary,

'These things happen in hotels,' she told me. 'Most likely a student prank. Nothing to worry about.'

I noticed though that the security guard stayed behind and began to take photographs of the damage right away.

I was uneasy. The trashing of the room was scarily similar to what had happened to my house in Dunoon. However, I needed somewhere to spend the night so I allowed myself and my bag to be taken to a large, well-appointed room on the second floor. I closed the curtains and went straight to bed. I was not expecting to fall asleep at all that night, but I did.

12

Waking early the next morning, I felt surprisingly refreshed and ready to continue the drive to my sister's house in Bungay. Deciding to set off before the roads got busy, I went down to the restaurant as soon as it opened, taking my jacket, shoulder bag and overnight bag with me so that I would not have to go back to my room for them after breakfast. Being one of the first customers I had my choice of seating so opted for a seat at the far end of the room facing the door, from where I could watch and see who else came in. It was silly really because those two men would surely not return to the restaurant after walking out so abruptly yesterday evening, but it still felt safer with the wall behind me and an open view of the rest of the room. And even if the mayhem in my room last night had been no more than a student prank as the hotel manager suggested, I thought it best not to linger in York before hitting the road to Bungay.

I ordered a full English breakfast to sustain me for the rest of the journey: muesli followed by bacon, eggs, sausage and black pudding, finished off with toast and marmalade and a cup of tea.

From my vantage point facing the door I observed each of my fellow breakfasters as they came into the restaurant. Not one of them struck me as a suspicious character and nor did they take the slightest notice of me.

Fortified by a good breakfast and delighted to discover that not only had I not been charged for my room, I had not been charged for my breakfast either, I left a generous tip on the table, put on my jacket, picked up my bags and set off for the car park.

The hotel car park was no longer packed with restaurant customer cars as it had been the previous evening, so it was easy enough to glance round and assure myself there was no light-coloured SUV parked there. There were no other people about either; in fact all was quiet. Nevertheless. I instinctively hurried to my blue Beetle, unlocked the door, threw my overnight bag and purse onto the passenger seat rather than wasting time opening the bonnet and slipped into the driving seat with a sigh of relief.

I was glad to get away from the hotel that morning. Despite the manager's reassurances. I didn't agree with her 'student prank' assessment of the previous evening. The way my hotel room had been trashed was too reminiscent of the treatment my house in Scotland had received.

The early morning traffic was light and the weather was fine so I made good time leaving York and headed for the A1 south, but I couldn't shake my uneasiness. I tried to stop thinking about the past few days and focus my thoughts instead on my sister and the things we enjoy doing together. It was a perfect time of the year to see the beautiful Suffolk countryside, painted so memorably by John Constable. In my mind I could see Gabriella's lovely garden too, the result of hard work by fingers far greener than mine.

Thinking of Gabriella however brought a new and very disturbing idea, something that had not occurred to me before. If I had been followed to York because the bogus policemen hadn't been able to find Captain Walker's package and letter in my house in Scotland, and since whoever searched my hotel room had also presumably been looking for them and had not found them there either, then I was possibly still being followed. What if I were followed to Bungay and as a result Gabriella's house should receive the same treatment as my own home and the hotel room in York? What if by going to stay with Gabriella I put her in danger too? Obviously I could not do that.

Instead of continuing my journey south, I left the A1 at Grantham, found a coffee shop near the railway station and sipped coffee while I thought the situation through. For the first time, I began to wonder what role my neighbour had played in all of this. He had arrived a few minutes early for the neighbourhood coffee morning on Wednesday and found me lying unconscious in my doorway. He'd dispatched the other neighbours when they arrived for coffee, saw me safely to hospital, and came to take me home the following day after I was discharged. It was his suggestion that I should go to stay elsewhere while the police complete their investigation. When I agreed and said I would go and stay with Gabriella, he dispatched me with all haste together with a packet of sandwiches and a bottle of water. What was his part in all this? I couldn't believe he was directly involved in whatever was going on with the package and letter, but I just had a feeling he knew more than he was telling me.

There were one or two things that didn't quite add up though. For example, it would not have been difficult for those two men to follow me to the hotel in York, but how did they learn my room number and then how did they gain access to the room? Second, why was one of them surprised to see me in the hotel if they had in fact followed me there? The hotel manager could possibly be right, that the room trashing had been no more than a student prank. Also, the two men changing their minds about eating in the restaurant may have had nothing to do with me. In fact, a case could be made that I had not been followed to York at all. Nevertheless I thought it prudent to telephone Gabriella and cancel the visit.

My sister Gabriella always did have a sense of the dramatic. She was absolutely thrilled by the idea of mystery and intrigue back in Dunoon and was completely unimpressed by my suggestion of potential danger. She couldn't wait to get involved.

'I tell you what, Aggie,' she said, 'I've got a friend who lives near the station in Cambridge. He won't mind me leaving my car at his place. If I set off right away, I can get a train from Cambridge to London and then get an East Coast main line train up to York. You drive back to York now and find a hotel somewhere near the station where we can stay the night. I'll join you when I arrive. I don't know the train times offhand but I'll get there eventually. I'll call you on your mobile when I get to York and get a taxi to wherever you are. Tomorrow we'll drive back to Dunoon in your car. And,' she added as if it were the clincher, 'I'll share the driving.'

Gabriella can still take me by surprise. While I was still digesting her knee-jerk proposition and considering its feasibility, she said brightly, 'Right then, that's settled. See you in York.' Then she rang off.

What else was there to do? I didn't have much of an alternate plan to offer. I had vaguely thought of touring in Wales, with or without Gabriella, until it was deemed safe for me to return home to Dunoon. I called her again to suggest this but there was no reply. Canny Gabriella knew me too well. She was not about to pick up the phone and be talked out of her plan.

13

It was still only mid-morning thanks to the early start from York. Per Gabriella's instructions I left the cafe in Grantham right away to hit the road back to York. Knowing it would be late afternoon or early evening before she would arrive, I considered the best way to fill the time. I could drive back via the motorway, which would be the quickest route, find a hotel in York and just wait there until she arrived or I could take a slower route back, stop for lunch on the way and have less of a wait for her arrival. I decided to go back via the motorway. York is a major tourist centre and it would be easier to find a hotel room earlier in the day than later. There would be plenty of opportunities to eat after that.

On arrival back at York, again per Gabriella's instructions I drove straight to the railway station and began to look for accommodation in that area. I spotted a small hotel near Micklegate Bar that looked promising and decided to try it. A narrow lane led off the main road to the hotel's car park behind the building. I drove in, parked my car, went into the hotel and enquired at the reception desk. I was in luck. The hotel was able to offer me a room for two for the night at a very reasonable rate. The only question now was how long it would be before Gabriella arrived. I was hungry and ready for a late lunch.

Belatedly I realised that it would have been smarter to take a slower route back from Grantham and stop for lunch on the way. It was probably not a good idea to go wandering out in the city as I had on the previous day. The two men I believed had followed me form Dunoon yesterday evening might still be in York. I certainly didn't want to risk them seeing me. It was just a pity that the hotel was too small to have its own restaurant. However there was a hospitality tray in the room with an electric kettle, tea and coffee bags, sachets of sugar and artificial sweetener, small cartons of UHT milk and a two small packages of shortbread biscuits. That would have to do. I made a cup of tea and unashamedly scoffed both packages of biscuits. Gabriella could go out and buy food for both of us when she arrived.

Predictably it was early evening before a taxi brought her to the hotel. By that time the benefit of the tea and shortbread biscuits had long worn off and my stomach was churning with hunger and anxiety.

Gabriella greeted me effusively as usual. 'Aggie! Lovely to see you! Great news! There's a fish and chip shop just outside the hotel. Let's go!'

'But I was going to stay inside.'

'Come on! I spotted it from the taxi as I arrived. I haven't eaten since you called this morning so I'm going straight out before I take my coat off. Aren't you coming? I do hope they have mushy peas too. Come on, you can watch me eat if you're not hungry yourself.'

My resolution vanished. Throwing caution to the winds and my jacket over my shoulders, I picked up my purse. What risk could there possibly be in going to a fish and chip shop just outside the hotel? If I'd known it was there, I'd have gone earlier myself.

'Come on then, Gabs,' I said happily. 'My treat, I haven't eaten either. By the way, lovely to see you again!' I gave her a hug. 'We can catch up on what's going on while we eat. Did you see if they have tables there or do we have to bring our chips back to the hotel and eat them here? It's all right if we do. We can make a cup of tea and sit at the table here.'

'I don't know if we can eat there or not, Aggie. I didn't see into the shop,' Gabriella replied. 'But let's go and find out.'

The fish and chip shop must have been a popular one because there was a small queue of people extending from the counter and round the room all the way to the doorway. As Gabriella and I joined the line I glanced round at the other customers, trying to assess how long we would have to wait.

Just in time I spotted the burly frames of

two men, one taller than the other, in the process of being served. They were standing in front of the counter with their backs towards us but I was in no doubt they were the same two men that had come into the hotel restaurant the previous evening. They were being asked if they wanted salt and vinegar on their orders. One of them was already pulling notes out of his wallet to pay. In another moment they could turn from the counter to go out of the door and see me standing in line there. Horrified, I stepped back out of the shop doorway as quickly and quietly as I could, pulling Gabriella back with me.

'Quick! Run!' I whispered.

Gabriella is quick on the uptake, I'll give her that. She rushed after me and waited until we were back in the safety of the hotel reception area to ask why.

'Aggie, what's going on? I'm starving and you've just made us lose our place in the queue.'

'I'll explain later,' I reassured her, 'but right now I can't go out there again. There were two men in the fish shop that mustn't see me. They were paying. You probably didn't notice them, both stocky and one taller than the other. Anyway, it means you'll have to go for our fish and chips by yourself and bring them back to eat in our room. Two fish for me please, and maybe get a bottle of ginger beer if they have one. Here's the money, I'm still paying,' I added, taking some notes from my purse.

'OK,' she agreed. 'But look, take my coat up to the room, I'm sweltered after all that running. I need a pocket for the cash though so I'll wear your jacket instead. That way I won't have to carry my purse as well as the fish and chips.'

I gave her my jacket, took her heavy tweed coat over my arm and went upstairs to our room to make a pot of tea to go with the fish and chips. I hung her coat up. It had been unnecessary to bring it but Gabriella always claims Scotland is cold, even in summer.

Over dinner in our room, I brought her up to speed on all that had happened over the past few days right up to the present. She was both horrified and fascinated.

'Wow, Aggie!' she exclaimed when I finished, 'I can see now why you rushed back from the fish shop. Anyway, you'll be pleased to know that I did a little sleuthing when I went for our fish and chips. I looked to see if those two men you described were still hanging around, just in case they had seen you in the shop.'

'Oh, thanks,' I replied. 'That was very thoughtful of you, but I daresay they'd be long gone. They were already paying for their order when I saw them.'

'Well,' said Gabriella smugly, 'they may have left the shop, but I did notice a light-coloured SUV parked on the road just beyond it with two men in it eating their fish and chips. They'd gone by the time I came out again though.'

'Did either of them look at you?'

'No, but really Aggie, why should they?'

'Well, we do look rather alike.'

'Look, don't worry,' she said reassuringly, 'they were far too busy stuffing their faces to pay any attention to passersby. Anyway, they'd gone by the time I left.'

'Maybe, but why were they parked there when you went back?' I wondered. 'I'm pretty sure I'd have noticed if an SUV had been parked outside the shop earlier, especially a light-coloured one.'

A disturbing thought struck me.

'Oh Gabs! What if they're staying in this hotel too?'

She sighed. 'Pull yourself together, Aggie,' she said firmly. 'It's highly unlikely they're staying here. Think about it. Why would anyone park on a double yellow line to eat their fish and chips if they could use the hotel car park right next to the fish shop? They could have brought their food indoors to eat, just as we did.'

I shook my head. 'I'm not sure Gabs. What if they did spot me and were waiting for me to go back to the fish shop so they could follow me to see where I'm staying. They'll still be thinking I have Captain Walker's correspondence. I've no idea where it is, but they don't know that.'

'Well,' Gabriella held up a knowing finger, 'I know just how to find out if they're here.'

She put on her coat. 'I'm going to check the hotel car park. Coming?'

'If they are staying in this hotel,' I said, 'we need to get away before they know I'm staying here as well. We'd better both go. We'll take our things with us, then if the SUV's in the car park we'll simply load up the car and take off.'

I was very worried but Gabriella was enjoying herself immensely. She slipped on her shoes, threw on her coat and grabbed her travel bag and purse.

'Right, come on Aggie, let's go. This is fun!'

I looked at my sister severely. 'This isn't a game, Gabs.'

'I know,' she said contritely, 'but I can't help enjoying it.'

Fortunately we were both travelling light. We put our handbags in our travel bags so as to be carrying only one bag each and managed to leave the hotel without attracting attention. I had already pre-paid for the room so we didn't need to check out.

It was beginning to get dark and the car park was only spottily lit. In fact the far end where I had left my car was almost completely dark. There were not many cars parked and no SUV of any colour.

'It looks as though we're OK to spend the night here after all,' I told Gabriella. 'But while we're out I'll just check that I locked the car.'

With no sense of urgency, we sauntered over to my blue Beetle, debating as we went whether we should go straight back to my house in Dunoon tomorrow or whether we should stay away until I'd received an 'all clear' message from Richard. Gabriella was pushing for going straight back to Dunoon, pointing out that that she had not brought enough clothes for a couple of weeks. She had packed only the necessities for a couple of nights, planning to use my laundry facilities and borrow anything more that was needed from my wardrobe.

'Don't forget,' she said, 'I had to pack in a hurry and only brought what I could carry easily on the train.'

This was true. She had dropped everything and set out to join me immediately when I'd called her from Grantham. The sooner I began to put my house to rights the better, and Gabriella would be a great help.

'OK,' I said, 'Dunoon it is. Let's have breakfast as soon as they begin to serve it in the morning, then get away from York as early as we can before the roads get busy.'

I pressed the handle of my car door to make sure that it was locked, then picked up my bag to go back into the hotel. As I did so, headlights beamed into the car park. Gabriella saw them too. Instinctively, without speaking, we both ducked down in the darkness behind my car to watch who came in. An SUV turned into one of the better lit parking slots about thirty feet away. Two heavyset men, one taller than the other, got out. We were well back from the main road and traffic noise, and they were not keeping their voices down so we heard their conversation clearly across the car park.

'Yer sure it were 'er then?'

'Oh aye, she were wearing that red jacket, just like yesterday when we saw 'er coming out of that 'otel. Easy to spot, like. It were lucky we were driving past.'

'Aye, an' even luckier that cleaner let us into 'er room. We turned the place upside down, but there were nowt there. I reckon she left it in 'er car. That's if it was
'er. Pity we don't know what car she's driving. You should 'ave remembered what kind of car she 'as. It were you that looked in 'er garage.'

'Well I remember it were the same blue colour as that one that acted funny coming into York. You know the one. It kept slowing down and speeding up. That were a blue Beetle. It gave me a right shock seeing 'er again in the 'otel last night.'
'Aye, that's if it was 'er that you saw.'

'Oh aye, I remembered 'er face. Nice like.'

'Yer sentimental sod! Anyway, 'ave a look round these cars and see if you think one of them is 'ers. It'll be a flashy one. They've got money in them 'ouses in Dunoon. Look for a red one.'

'There's a blue car up at the end there but it's just an old banger. Still, we could get the license number. Ave yer got yer glasses?'

'No, but we don't need 't number. We can just go inside t'otel and ask if she's there.'

'You can. I'm not.'

'Come on, yer daft bugger.'

The two men strode towards the hotel. I didn't need to tell Gabriella what to do. The minute the hotel door closed after them we leaped into the Beetle. I left my headlights off until we exited the car park onto the road. We filled up with petrol on the outskirts of York and didn't stop again until we reached the Glasgow airport turnoff from the M8 five hours later. I knew we would miss the last ferry from Gourock to Dunoon that night, so we checked into one of the airport hotels.

14

We filled up the car at the airport and drove on to Dunoon the next morning. During the 20-minute ferry crossing from Gourock to Dunoon I warned Gabriella again of the extent of the damage in the house. She was not at all perturbed.

'There's nothing that can't be put right, Aggie,' she declared confidently. 'We'll inspect each room, assess the damage and list what needs to be done.'

There is no point in arguing with Gabriella. She always was bossy, so I kept quiet. Let her see for herself!

'By the way,' she said casually, 'tell me about this interesting neighbour of yours. Is there something going on between you?'

Gabriella always did jump to conclusions.

'Don't be silly,' I said. I knew exactly what was in her mind. She's a bit of a flirt. She said no more but I could just about hear her mind ticking.

Back home, Gabriella was eager to take charge, so I said, 'You go on into the house while I unpack the car. Put the kettle on for a cup of tea while you're at it. That's if you can find the kettle!'

'Will do!' she called cheerfully, disappearing into the house.

I started to collect things out of the car. I took the empty water bottle and sandwich wrappings from two days ago to the recycle bin by the gate, then went back to collect the coats and bags to take into the house. I hated to think of all the clearing, cleaning and repairs that would have to be done, but it had to be faced.

I closed the lid on the car bonnet and was about to carry our things into the house when Gabriella burst through the kitchen door, white faced and obviously very distressed. I was surprised to see her so affected by the state of the house.

'Oh Aggie,' she wailed, 'Aggie, Aggie, have you had episodes like this before?'

I was puzzled. 'No, of course I haven't. Why are you so upset? I did warn you what to expect when you went into the house, and you heard those two thugs in the car park in York talking about the hotel break-in.'

'It's all right, dear.' Gabriella came to the car and put an arm round me. 'Let me help you carry our things into the house. I've made a pot of tea and found some nice chocolate biscuits, so you come in and sit down. Are you warm enough? The house may be a bit cold for you. I'll turn the heating up if you tell me how to do it. Maybe after a cup of tea you should lie down for a while.'

I was mystified by this syrupy solicitude.

If I had been showing signs of distress, which of course I wasn't, I would have expected her to tell me to pull myself together rather than offer a chair and chocolate biscuits. I wondered if things inside the house were even worse than I remembered. Back on the ferry Gabriella had implied she was ready to deal singlehandedly with the mess, so why was she distressed now?

'I didn't know,' she went on, 'you'd been doing so much to the house. It's exhausted you completely. No wonder you got it all mixed up in your mind with that hotel incident.'

Puzzled, but not wishing to upset her further, I allowed myself to be led gently into the house. To my astonishment, I was greeted not by the chaos I had left behind two days ago but a sparkling, gleaming kitchen. Everything looked brand new: the range, dishwasher and microwave, the counters, cupboards and drawers. The damaged table and broken chairs had been replaced with what looked like brand new furniture. The window was sparkling, and healthy plants bloomed in matching ceramic pots on the window sill. The floor was clean and shining. Now I don't like to think of myself as a slouch, but this was way beyond my normal level of housekeeping.

'Goodness gracious!' I exclaimed in surprise. 'Richard must have cleaned the kitchen for me. How kind of him! And in just two days too! What a great job he's done, it looks better than new!’

Gabriella looked at me sadly. ‘That’s because it is all new, dear. Look, the bills are here on the counter.’ She waved a sheaf of paper at me. ‘All marked ‘paid’.’

I gaped at her. Richard had really gone overboard getting all this done without my authorisation.

‘You must have made arrangements a while back, dear, so that you could have the work done while you were staying with me. And then you must have forgotten all about it,’ she continued sadly. ‘I thought previously that you were beginning to forget things. But I must say, Aggie, your contractors are fantastic. It’s amazing to me how they could time their jobs to fit in with one another and be finished in two days.’ She shook her head. ‘But they obviously did because the dates are here on the invoices. I looked through them while you were still in the garage. I just wish I could get service like that where I live.’

Gabriella always was nosy. Fancy looking through other peoples’ bills! I tried to tell her that I had never made any such arrangements, in fact could not possibly have done so. It was only two days ago that I’d telephoned her on Richard’s recommendation to arrange a visit to Bungay and I had set off less than an hour after calling her. But my sister was just not listening. She was far too busy inspecting the utility room which leads off the kitchen.

'Yes,' she was saying, 'I'd have chosen that washer and dryer combination too. The newer ones are so much better and use less energy. I like that freezer as well. And you've put the same cupboards and counters in the utility room as the kitchen and carried the floor covering through both rooms. Well done, Aggie!'

I followed her dumbly into the utility room and could only stare at the new cupboards, counters and the floor covering matching those in the kitchen.

'You made extremely good arrangements,' continued psychiatrist Gabriella, slipping seamlessly from her sorrowful sister persona to that of professional diagnostician, 'but somehow you've forgotten all about it. I dare say you took on too much, and became overwrought. Your mind must have filled the memory gap with that story about letters and packages and window cleaners and men following you.'

I stared at her. Was such a thing possible? Surely not in my case! I wasn't really worried by what she was saying though, because I knew that Gabriella would realise her mistake as soon as she saw the rest of the house. Richard must have ordered all the work in the kitchen and I could sort that out with him later but in the meantime Gabriella must be sorted out and I thought I knew an easy way to do it.

I finished my tea and said, 'The kitchen does look lovely, Gabs, but maybe I should lie down for a while as you suggest.' I turned away to hide my smile as I added, 'We'll have to make the bed first though.'

Gabriella's concern returned when I said that, but I didn't care. It served her right for that stupid diagnosis. I allowed her to escort me gently to my bedroom.

What a shock awaited me there! I thought I was beyond surprise after seeing the kitchen, but lo and behold, the bedroom was not in the chaotic state I expected. It was just as immaculate as the kitchen. The bed was neatly made up with a new quilt and a teddy bear sitting at the head. The bedroom furniture gleamed and a tell-tale scent of polish lingered. The only things out of their customary places were a few ornaments. I opened the wardrobe door. My clothes hung neatly on the rails but each garment was covered by a plastic sheath sporting a dry cleaners' tag.

'Look,' said Gabriella. 'Look what a thorough spring clean you did. Not just the kitchen, you sent all your clothes to the cleaners as well.'

This was not right. There were other things about the room too that I hadn't noticed immediately as my attention had been focused on the bed and furniture. There was a new carpet on the floor and the door and the rest of the woodwork had been repainted. In fact, I could now detect a lingering smell of paint as well as furniture polish. The en-suite was similarly immaculate with a new set of rose-coloured towels. It was all too much.

‘Gabs,’ I told her, ‘believe me, I had nothing to do with all this. Either I’m in the middle of a fantastic dream or a magic wand has been waved over the house.’

I certainly wasn’t about to accept her diagnosis of impending dementia. The rest of the house would surely tell the story.

‘I’ll tell you what, let’s look at the other rooms. They were all turned upside down too.’

‘All right, but after that I think you should lie down,’ Gabriella replied firmly.

I had no intention of lying down but there was no point in arguing. The facts would speak for themselves when we went to look at the other rooms in the house. With respect to the bedroom, I thought that Richard’s neighbourliness was going a bit overboard, particularly since he hadn’t checked with me to see how much I could afford to pay before ordering all these refurbishments, but it was thoughtful of him. After all, the kitchen and the bedroom are the most heavily used rooms in a house. I was sure he would not have bothered to do anything about the other rooms in my bungalow: the second bedroom, the guest bathroom, the living room, and the study which doubles as a dining room on the rare occasion it is needed.

‘This,’ I told Gabriella, as I opened the door of the second bedroom with a flourish, ‘will be your room when …’

‘Oh Aggie, it’s lovely!’ she exclaimed, rushing in, delighted with what she saw. Indeed it was. Furniture polished, paint and a new carpet, and another patchwork quilt with pillows that I had certainly never seen before had transformed my very ordinary-looking spare bedroom into a most inviting one. No wonder Gabriella was in raptures about sleeping there.

At least her cheerful spirit had returned at the sight of her room. I just hoped my bank account would stand it. Thinking about it, the kitchen and bedrooms were a vast improvement. Richard had done a much better job than I would have done and it would have taken me a lot longer. I still had to persuade Gabriella that I was of sane mind though.

I was sure Richard would not have attempted anything in the living room or my study. Apart from anything else, there would not have been time do more than he had already. With this in mind, I invited Gabriella to inspect the other rooms. First I opened the door to my study/dining room. Not a stick of furniture was out of place and once again the tell-tale aromas of furniture polish, paint and new carpet. My laptop computer was on the desk, plus a new mouse and pad, and an elegant holder for pens and pencil, paper clips and the like was strategically placed at the back of the desk.

'My!' said Gabriella, 'I'm impressed. You keep your things a lot tidier than you used to, Aggie. Look.'

She grabbed the bunch of pencils, all the

same length, out of their compartment in the elegant holder. I knew better by this time than to deny any previous knowledge of them.

'All the same length and all with lovely points,' she went on. 'I'll have to get a sharpener like this one myself.'

I followed her gaze to the shiny red electric pencil sharpener sitting on the cabinet beside my desk where I keep important papers. That pencil sharpener was something else I had never seen before. I was getting increasingly worried about the cost of everything.

'Well,' I said, shaking my head in bewilderment, 'there's only the living room left. Let's go and look. You never know your luck, maybe it's been done too.'

Yes, the living room was indeed re-carpeted and repainted, just like the other rooms. I was relieved to see my furniture had not been damaged because I had spent a lot of time and effort choosing it after I moved into the house. As in the other rooms, the telltale scent of furniture polish lingered.

'What a lovely house you have, Aggie!' Gabriella enthused, rushing into the room. 'With this fantastic view too.'

She walked straight over to the bay window to enjoy the panoramic view, as most people do when they come into my house. She sighed as she looked up and down the water below and across to the mountains beyond. Suddenly, she signalled me to join her at the window. Something out there had attracted her attention.

'Aggie, I can see your next door neighbour's sun deck from this side of the window. There are two men out there sitting in chairs and drinking something from cans. Let me get my specs on. They're in my bag on the kitchen table. I need to get a better look to be sure.'

She rushed into the kitchen to retrieve her glasses then rushed back to the window. Gabriella always was inquisitive.

'Gabs, don't be so nosy,' I said. 'That's Richard Carter's house, the neighbour I told you about. He has every right to be out there with his friends. I do hope he doesn't see you peering out at him.'

By this time Gabriella had her glasses on and was staring intently.

'Aggie,' she said uncertainly, 'I don't know what your neighbour looks like, but one of those two is George.'

It couldn't be George. George is Gabriella's son. During our drive north, when I asked her how her family was getting on she told me proudly that he was on assignment in Hong Kong. I looked for the binoculars that I keep handy by the window to watch sea birds and passing ships. But they were nowhere to be seen in my immaculate, newly furbished living room.

'Are those distance glasses?' I asked Gabriella.

'Yes.' She handed them to me. 'Have a look

yourself.'

I looked. Sure enough, Richard was sitting on his sun deck chatting to my nephew, George Chester.

15

'Angelina!' Richard dropped the paper he was holding. His face registered surprise rather than pleasure at the sight of Gabriella and me on the steps to his deck. 'I thought you were off to stay with your sister for a couple of weeks. Why have you come back?'

George, turning towards us, was even more surprised to see his mother with me. 'Mum! Aunt Aggie! How did you two get here?' Not much of a welcome there either.

Gabriella was disconcerted. 'And I'm happy to see you too, George,' she snapped. Gabriella always did have a short fuse.

'Oh Mum, it's great to see you again, of course it is. You too, Aunt Aggie.' He gave us both a hug and a kiss. 'I didn't mean it like that. Of course I'm happy to see you. I was just surprised. Dick told me Aunt Aggie left here two days ago to stay with you in Bungay for a while.'

George spoke cheerfully enough but I thought he looked worried. I wondered why.

'We just weren't expecting you Mum.' he repeated. 'That's why I'm surprised to see you.'

'No, it's very clear you weren't expecting to see us.' Gabriella was far from satisfied. 'I wasn't expecting to see you here either, George. You told me you were in Hong Kong. Why did you say you were in Hong Kong when you're here in Dunoon.'

The morning was getting more and more unreal. I stood by the balcony rail forcing myself to breathe slowly. Coming home to find my house completely refurbished had been a real shock. Then my nephew George, whom Gabriella assured me was in Hong Kong, turns up in Dunoon. Why was he here and what was his connection with my next-door neighbour? And why the cool reception from both of them? I expected surprise from Richard and that he would ask why I hadn't stayed away while the break-in was being investigated. But surely a little more warmth from both of them would have been in order.

'By the way, Aunt Aggie,' George turned from his agitated mother to me, 'what do you think to your house? Did we do a good job? We tried to put everything back as it should be. It's a lovely house by the way.'

Here was yet another surprise. My nephew George had been involved in putting my house to rights!

I had a poignant moment watching Gabriella's face as the implication of George's question struck and she realised I had not been deluded about the state of my house! So much for her diagnosis concerning my mental health or lack thereof.

To her credit, Gabriella blushed. 'Oh Aggie!' she gasped contritely. 'You're all right after all! To think I didn't believe you about the house! I'm so sorry.'

It was George's turn to look mystified. Very satisfying!

Richard reappeared on the deck to say, 'I've made coffee, let's all go indoors. We've a lot to talk about.' He nodded to George. 'We can sit by the window.'

By the window was fine with me. I didn't care where we sat. I just wanted to know what was going on. I wanted to know how and why my house had been so completely transformed in the two days I was away. I was not unhappy with the result, quite the reverse. I just worried about the cost. I had insurance of course but surely a few nasty spills wouldn't justify re-carpeting throughout the house and new floor coverings in the kitchen and utility room, bathrooms and corridor. Then there were the new appliances, the cooker, the microwave the dishwasher, the washer, the dryer and the freezer. Were they really so badly scratched or dented that they needed replacing? Had photographs been taken of the damage? There were new items of furniture too, the kitchen table and chairs. I was desperate to know how it would affect my bank balance. Would I need to withdraw my entire retirement savings to pay for it? What if my retirement savings were not enough?

'Don't look so gloomy, Angelina,' Richard said heartily as he handed be a mug of strong black coffee. He has one of those very expensive coffee making machines that grinds its own beans and brews any amount of coffee to order. I always thought it a ridiculous extravagance for a man living on his own, but that was his business and it certainly made wonderful coffee.

'Richard,' I told him, gratefully accepting the coffee, 'please don't get me wrong, you and George have done fantastic job on my house, and I'm very grateful to you, but I'm really worried about the cost of it all. Please tell me how much I'm in your debt.'

'Oh,' he shook his head, 'you don't owe me anything. George did it all. I had nothing to do with it. I have to say though, I was very impressed when he showed me the result.'

I looked at George and then at Gabriella. George looked rather smug. As for Gabriella, 'gobsmacked' is the word that comes to mind.

I had assumed Richard had organised the clean-up and transformation of my house and that George knew about it because Richard had shown it off to him. Now it transpired the reverse was true. George had organised the work and shown it off to Richard. It was definitely time for some answers.

My first question was why George had been in my house in the first place. He must have been inside ir to know about the damage. Come to think of it, I know I locked the door carefully before I left for Bungay. What was he doing there when, according to Gabriella, he should have been in Hong Kong? And how had he managed to do the clean-up and get all the work and replacements done in just two days? I would have expected it to take a lot longer – weeks or even months.

'George,' I said firmly, 'you've got some explaining to do.'

'Later, Aunt Aggie, I promise, and by the way, forget the cost.'

George didn't sit down with the rest of us. He took his coffee to the window, and stood looking down on the road below. Out on the deck earlier I had been aware that he kept glancing at the road but thought nothing of it. Now I was very curious to know what he was watching for.

Now Gabriella is not the only one who knows a bit of psychology. Rather than ask George outright and risk being fobbed off, I opened the line of questioning obliquely, saying conversationally, 'George, I'm surprised you didn't see your Mum and myself arriving while you were sitting out on the deck. We drove right past here.'

'Well,' George replied, falling neatly into my trap, 'there hasn't been a lot of traffic along the road this morning, mostly local cars and delivery vans. I would have spotted you if I'd known what car you're driving nowadays.'

So they had been watching for something. I knew it.

'I did see a blue Beetle go past,' Richard said. 'It just didn't enter my head that it could be yours. I wasn't expecting you back for another week or two.'

'Aunt Aggie!' George exclaimed, 'Surely you're not still driving that old blue Beetle. You've had it for years. It must be ready for the scrap heap.'

I didn't think that merited an answer. There is nothing wrong with my car.

After sipping our coffee in silence for a minute or two, George said, 'I think we'd better tell them what's going on, Dick, just to put them on their guard.'

I could almost feel my ears prick.

Richard nodded. 'I think so. By the way, Angelina, did you lock your door before you came over?'

'No,' I replied. 'I didn't bother to lock up because we only came over for a few minutes to say hello.'

'And to find out what George is doing here.' Gabriella added.

Recovered from the shock of finding George in Dunoon and conveniently forgetting her misgivings about my sanity, Gabriella was ready to demand explanations too.

Richard nodded. 'I'll keep watch here while you take care of Angelina's door.'

What was going on? George was watching the road and Richard was concerned about my door being locked. Where did George fit into the picture? What he was doing in my house? Why had he organised its restoration? What was the connection between him and my neighbour, a retiree like myself?

I waited for George's return. I thought it would be unfair to grill Richard after all his kindness but was quite prepared to give my nephew the third degree. I figured I'd get better results by leading in gently though, so when George returned I thanked him for going to lock my door and asked casually, 'Did you find the key all right? It would be in my purse in the kitchen.'

'No need.' He waved a key at me. 'I still have this one. You gave it to me that time Mum and I came to stay when you first moved in. Don't you remember?' I did recall the occasion. 'Oh yes,' I said. 'I do remember. I had a dental appointment that day and needed some groceries too, so I gave you a key to lock up in case you decided to go out before I got back. I didn't realise you still had it though.'

Gabriella intervened, changing the subject before I could say any more about the key. She doesn't like other people criticising her son.

'You've a good memory, Aggie.'

I said sweetly, 'So you think my memory's OK then, Gabs?'

'I really am sorry.'

She had the grace to blush again. The two men, realising they were missing some nuance, looked from one to the other of us, waiting for an explanation. But twins don't let each other down in public. Not these twins anyway.

'Just a private joke between us,' I told them, smiling to myself.

'Right, then let's get down to business,' said Richard, walking over to the window to join George. 'It might be best if you start by telling us why you came back, Angelina. I assume you did so for a reason, not just on a whim.'

'Yes, I'll be glad to tell you,' I replied, and I did. I told them about the SUV I thought might be following me on the road to York. I told them about the two men who came into the restaurant, looked at me and left abruptly, and of the dreadful state I found my room in when I took my bag up from the car after dinner. I told them how the hotel manager didn't want to call the police, and instead just brushed it off as a student prank and gave me another room instead. I told them how I decided to get away from York early the next morning, in case those two men were on the look-out for me. I told them that although I didn't see anyone following me on the road, I became increasingly uneasy, so stopped at Grantham and called Gabriella.

Gabriella took over. 'I could tell that Aggie was worried about something and needed moral support so I took the train up to York. When I got there she told me about her house and the hotel in York being trashed. She didn't want to risk the same thing happening to my house in Bungay.'

Gabriella always did like to appear the heroine. Still, it had been good of her to drop everything and come as soon as I called so I didn't comment.

'Shall I tell them about the two men and the fish and chips, Aggie?' Gabriella was clearly itching to do so and I thought it would be a good idea to hear her take on the incident anyway.

'Yes, go ahead.' I nodded.

Gabriella is actually very good at marshalling facts. She described how we went for fish and chips and I spotted the two men paying for their order at the counter and how we hurried back into the hotel, hoping they hadn't recognised me.

'Wait a minute,' George interrupted. 'Are you talking about the two men Aunt Aggie encountered in York? Were you sure of that, Aunt Aggie?'

'Of course she's sure,' his mother snapped impatiently. She continued to relate how she went back to the chippy alone and saw the two men eating theirs in an SUV parked outside the shop.

'I didn't think they noticed me,' she said, 'but they must have seen me and thought I was Aggie. People do say we look alike and I was wearing her red jacket. Anyway, as a safety precaution we decided not to stay in York any longer. We took our things down to the car and put them in the bonnet, but just as we were getting into the car ourselves, that SUV turned into the car park.' She paused for dramatic effect. 'Fortunately, it was dark by then and the car park wasn't well lit, so we ducked down and hid behind the car. We overheard enough of what they were saying to know that they were definitely looking for Aggie. One of them said it was a pity they didn't know what car Aggie was driving and the other thought she would be driving a posh one so they didn't look twice at the Beetle. It probably helped that it needed a good wash. Anyway, they went into the hotel to find out if she was staying there and that's when we got away.'

'And that,' I finished up, 'is why we came straight back here. I don't know how they followed me to York if they didn't know what car I was in, but there they were in the hotel restaurant. I know it's all tied in somehow with that package and letter. That's when it all started. Did Richard tell you about that, George?'

George ignored my question, continuing to look out of the window, but I wasn't about to be let the matter go.

'George, just what is your connection to Richard? He and the local police are the only ones who knew about the break-in so you must have heard about it from one or the other. You didn't just wander into my house, notice it had been ransacked and decide to give your auntie as lovely surprise by putting it all right again.'

Gabriella nodded agreement.

‘Particularly when you were supposed to be in Hong Kong,’ she said, waspishly.

‘Of course it was a wonderful surprise,’ I added hastily.

George looked from the window to Richard.

‘You or me, Dick?’

Richard nodded. ‘It’s your story, George. You tell it.’

16

'Well,' George began, 'Dick and I have known each other for a long time.'

Richard nodded.

George continued, 'We used to work together. Actually Dick was my boss. Mum, I've always told you I work for the government, and I do, but in a special department. My job involves national security. We investigate suspicious activity around sensitive government issues. Our teams can be sent anywhere in the world. I'm not going to get any more specific than that.'

He nodded meaningfully to Gabriella who was ready to pepper him with questions.

'Yes, Mum, I really was in Hong Kong recently but that's all finished.'

That silenced her for the time being.

'Anyway,' George continued, 'I took over our group when Dick retired. I was given an assignment up here a couple of weeks ago. I got in touch with Dick because I knew he would know the area well. Then I discovered he actually lives next door to you, Aunt Aggie.'

'I see,' I said. 'So you decided to visit me

at the same time as Richard and that's when you discovered the state my house was in. But that had nothing to do with you, George. Richard and I figured the damage was done by two bogus policemen. We're pretty sure they were looking for a package and a letter that were mistakenly sent to my address. It was nothing at all to do with you, so why on earth did you feel responsible for clearing it all up? Like I said, I'm delighted with the result, but I do need to know the cost and then I shall have to work out how to pay for it.'

'Ah,' George hesitated and looked again towards Richard. 'The package and letter. Dick?'

Richard turned from the window and nodded again.

'The fact is, Aunt Aggie,' George continued, 'I'm the one who caused all the trouble with the package and letter. They were part of an investigation I was conducting. And as you've already realised, they were the reason you were attacked and your house turned upside down looking for them. It's only right that you should be properly compensated. You don't owe a penny for the work done. And if we've overlooked anything that still needs doing, just let me know. Also, if you'd like to see a specialist about your head injury we'll arrange that too.'

'But how did you manage to get all the work done so quickly?' Gabriella asked.

George grinned. 'Our organisation has a peripatetic mop-up crew we can call on. It's shared by several departments of course and isn't needed very often, not by us at any rate. This is the first time I've had to use them. Did they do a good job?'

'Excellent job,' I replied. 'I'm very grateful to you for doing it and unimaginably relieved about the cost, but I still have questions. I want to know more about the package and letter. There was nothing special about them except that they came to the wrong address and both disappeared before I was able to return them. I'm guessing they're important because people are still looking for them. I'm sure those two men in York were after them. So I think I deserve an explanation.'

'Well,' George mused, 'the perpetrator is safely under lock and key now so maybe I can tell you a little of what it was about.'

He looked at us sternly. 'Of course, this information must go no further. You do understand, Aunt Aggie? Mum?'

We nodded.

'Of course,' I replied.

'Neither of us would ever breathe a word,' Gabriella added.

'Come on, ' she urged as he hesitated, 'for heaven's sake, don't keep us in suspense.'

'Well,' George continued carefully, 'My team came up here to deal with a leak of classified information from one of the military bases. The base had been running tests on some new top secret defence technology.'

Gabriella and I stared. This was George, her son, my nephew doing James Bond stuff! And we thought he simply had a desk job that involved the occasional trip overseas!

He continued, 'Information was being leaked using social media. I decided the quickest way to discover the source of the leaks would be to arrange a temporary glitch in the electronic data system at the military base, so that none of the staff could get access to the electronic files and would have to go back to old-fashioned paper shuffling for a while. Paper has to be copied and handled manually, so it's slower and easier to monitor. The existence of the leak was common knowledge at the base so it was no surprise when my team arrived to investigate. Only the CO knew that we were responsible for the computer glitch though.'

'Surely everyone at the base would have connected you with the glitch,' Gabriella interjected. 'I certainly would have if I'd been working there. Look, a team of investigators arrives to investigate leaks from the database and simultaneously the database is shut down! Of course people would make the connection.'

'You're right, Mum, and that's why we arranged for the glitch to hit the base a week ahead. We wanted the paper shuffling system to be in place before we arrived.'

'Oh right, good thinking.' Gabriella was eager for more. 'Anyway, did the paper shuffling help you discover the information leaker?'

'As a matter of fact it did, very quickly in fact. Everything's back to normal at the base now.'

George glanced questioningly at Richard, who nodded yet again.

' Unfortunately,' he continued, 'the scheme triggered local criminal activity, so although the investigation is over at the base, I'm still up here helping to mop up. Does that explain everything?'

'Absolutely not!' I, the victim of the 'local criminal activity' exclaimed. 'It doesn't even begin!'

'You're not going to fob us off like that, George,' Gabriella added firmly. 'Your aunt has been attacked and may still be in serious danger and we want to know why. We want to know who sent the package and letter to her house. I'm sure you know. We want to know why the package and letter are so important that Aggie was attacked on her own doorstep and her house ransacked by people looking for them. Stop being pompous. Tell us exactly what happened.'

George looked helplessly at Richard.

'Dick?'

'Your decision, George,' Richard shrugged, 'You're in charge now. For what it's worth I think it might be safer if you tell them what's happening.'

George nodded.

17

'I never imagined sending the package and letter to you would cause a problem Aunt Aggie,'

'Well, you were wrong about that, weren't you.' I said.

Gabriella was not about to have me criticise her son. 'Calm down, Aggie,' she snapped. 'Let George explain. He obviously had a very good reason or he wouldn't have sent them. You always did jump in,' she added, glaring at me.

I didn't want to snap back at her in front of Richard, so I just said nonchalantly, 'I'm listening George.'

'I'm sorry, Aunt Aggie. Let me explain what happened, OK? As you can imagine, security is very tight at the base and even more so in the advanced weapons research unit. Only a handful of senior staff have access to the complex security codes. That narrowed our list of suspects right away.

'The unit is housed in a separate building at the base. There is a guarded entry into a lobby with lockers and racks where coats, bags, briefcases, papers, etc., must be left. Security guards at the entry to the work room make sure nothing is carried in or out.

'The work room is a large open area with no partitions between desks. Four smaller rooms lead off the left hand side. The two middle ones are meeting rooms with floor to ceiling glass walls. The door in the far corner opens to the lavatories and the first room, the one close to the entrance – also with a glass wall – is a secure mail room. The CO took us in and introduced us to the staff so everyone in the room knew why we were there. He emphasised that we too were required to comply with all security measures.

'My colleague and I each took a desk in the far corner, one either side of the door leading to the lavatories, with a clear view across the whole room. Likewise, everybody working in the room could see us. Staff going to the lavatories would have to walk past either my desk or my colleague's and in so doing would be able to see clearly whatever was on our desks.

'We anticipated that nothing criminal would be attempted while we were there but that the perpetrator would be extremely interested in the progress of our investigation. My plan was to bait a trap for the perpetrator to identify himself.'

'So what was the trap?' Gabriella always did like to come straight to the point.

George once again glanced at Richard, then continued. 'As I told you, staff are checked to make sure they take nothing out with them. In addition, all outgoing mail has to go unsealed to the mail room for vetting before leaving the base.

'The first day we sat at our desks just watching everyone in the room. To begin with, we wanted to spook the perpetrator. My colleague would occasionally come over to my desk and whisper to me, looking meaningfully round the room. I would nod gravely and look carefully round the room too. We repeated this charade a couple of times over the course of the day and did the same thing a second day. By then all the staff were getting uncomfortable. You could feel the tension in the room.

'Mid-morning on the third day I took a pen, a wad of paper, a manila folder and a package mailer out of my desk drawer and arranged them on my desk. Just to make sure I had the attention of anyone interested in what I was doing, I dropped a few papers on the floor and made a great show of picking them up. I wrote carefully on several sheets taking my time. Then I made another show of checking, sorting and numbering the pages, placing them in the manila folder and stuffing the folder into the package mailer.

I addressed the package very clearly using a black marker pen to Captain John Walker at your address Aunt Aggie. I had to use a legitimate address so as not to raise questions in the mail room. I pushed the package to the back of my desk and left it there in full view of anyone walking past while I went to the lavatory. My colleague watched to see if anyone walked past my desk while I was gone. I met one of the staff members going into the lavatory as I was leaving. I glanced at my colleague. He gave a slight nod and I took the package straight to the mailroom.'

'So that's where the package came from,' I said. 'But what about the letter? That arrived a day after the package.'

'Probably the package got picked up soon after I took it to the mailroom,' George said. 'But the letter must have missed that day's outgoing mail. Anyway, towards the end of the morning my colleague took pen, paper and an envelope out of his desk drawer and began to write. Like me, he took plenty of time, as though thinking carefully before committing words to paper. He folded the single sheet of paper carefully, body language suggesting the contents were important, put the sheet of paper in the envelope and addressed it also to Captain John Walker, once again at your address, Aunt Aggie.

'The mailroom is locked while its staff go to the base canteen for lunch. However, outgoing mail can still be posted through a chute in the glass wall to a table below. My colleague waited until the mailroom was locked then took his letter there. He made a great show of trying the door, then, with every appearance of exasperation, posted it through the chute and left the building. I stayed at my desk. For the best part of an hour none of the remaining staff showed any interest in the letter. Just before the mailroom staff returned, the man I met earlier going into the lavatories posted his own package through the mailroom chute and peered through the glass wall to the table below. He was arrested on suspicion as he left the building.

'I was told later that he had admitted to accepting money for putting classified information on the internet in order to pay off gambling debts. I'm not the only one who didn't believe that story and there will have to be further investigation into the case but that isn't my department's responsibility.'

Gabriella and I must have looked surprised because George shrugged and said, 'Yes, it was a bit of an anti-climax really, but our work was done. We'd identified the source of the leaks. Our responsibility ended there. There was nothing more for us to do at the base except to submit our report. I released my colleague to go and spend time with his family. I just needed to stay in the area long enough to intercept Captain John Walker's package and letter at your house within the next couple of days.

'Believe me, Aunt Aggie, I wasn't planning to involve you. I couldn't risk phoning you from the base, so I came to Dunoon to tell you to expect the package and letter and ask you to hold them for me. I planned on telling you that I was attending a meeting in Glasgow and gave our London office your address to forward my mail as I hoped to spend a few days here with you after the meeting. I would explain that I'd had a message from our London office that they had inadvertently forwarded Captain Walker's mail here and my mail to his address.'

I sighed. 'And I daresay I'd have believed you, George. What went wrong?'

'Yes,' echoed Gabriella, 'what went wrong?'

'Well,' It was George's turn to sigh. 'I had at least a day to kill before either of them would be delivered. The meeting in Glasgow being a fiction, and knowing my ex-colleague Dick retired somewhere in these parts, I phoned and asked if he'd like to get together. He invited me to come and stay for a few days and gave me his address. That's when I discovered you were next-door neighbours. Serendipity? I didn't tell Dick of our relationship because I didn't want to trigger a social visit and possibly awkward questions. Therefore, I had to remove the package and letter before you started an inconvenient chain of enquiry.'

'So, George, I'm guessing you took them,' I prompted, eager to get to the nub of the matter. He really could be long-winded. 'How did you do it without me seeing you?'

'Well, you were out when the package arrived. I saw the carrier ring your doorbell then leave it by the front door. I couldn't retrieve it immediately, because a couple of your neighbours were chatting just outside your gate and would have seen me. They were still there when you arrived back carrying some bags and a potted plant. You put them down while you unlocked the door and then you spotted the package and picked it up. I guessed you put it down on the hall table because you came straight out to pick up your shopping. Then I had a stroke of luck. A couple of minutes later your garage door opened and you came out with a spade in one hand and the potted plant in the other and disappeared round the side of house. I nipped over the fence, went into your house through the open garage door, found the package on the hall table, and nipped smartly back over the fence.'

I looked at George's long legs. Mine would never have nipped smartly over any fence.

'Hmm,' I frowned. 'And what about the letter? That didn't arrive until the next morning.'

'No, that was a bit more tricky. A couple of window cleaners turned up right after the postal delivery. One of them wasn't even working. He just sat down at the side of your garage and pulled a book out of his backpack. He looked like a student. The other lad spent more time carrying a ladder from window to window and climbing up and down than actually washing windows. I wondered why he needed a ladder. He could easily have reached your windows with an extension pole. Anyway, while the one was busy with his books and the other had taken his ladder to the other side of the house you came out of the door.

You looked around, presumably for the window cleaner. You saw he wasn't there and went round the house to look for him, leaving your front door open. I fairly flew over the fence, grabbed the letter from the hall table and made it back to Dick's only seconds before you reappeared.

But once I'd got the package and letter back, the last thing I wanted was for you to spot me and make the connection. So, when Dick called from his study to say he was about to drive into Glasgow and invited me along, I was very happy to go with him. I thought I might go straight on to the airport but Dick persuaded me to stay another day. As things turned out it's a good thing he did.'

I stared at Richard, aghast at his complicity. 'You knew what was going on, Richard. Why didn't you trust me and make this daft nephew of mine tell me what he was doing? I could have helped.'

'No, Auntie, you've got it wrong,' George intervened. 'Dick didn't know anything about the package and letter. When I called him, he invited me to stay with him for a few days and I was glad to take him up on it. When he told me his address it sounded kind of familiar but it wasn't until I arrived that I realised he was your next-door neighbour. I didn't tell him I'd used your address for the investigation at the base. Need to know only, you see. I planned to get the package and letter back without involving Dick.'

I looked at Richard for confirmation. 'Is that true?'

He turned from the window. 'Yes, it's true. I wasn't involved until I came to your house for coffee the next day and found you unconscious in the doorway.' He turned back to the window. 'I can't tell you how sorry I am about that.'

'Well,' I replied, somewhat mollified, 'I suppose it wasn't your fault. But when did George finally tell you about his involvement?'

'Ah,' Richard was still on watch at the window, 'that was when he saw you being carried into the ambulance on a stretcher. He got the shock of his life. Deserved it too. He got another shock after the ambulance left, when I took him into your house to show him the damage. That's when he told me about the package and letter and divulged the fact that you are related.'

Gabriella was speechless.

'Right,' I said. 'So, getting back to the story, George, you must have seen Peggy Browne come to the door, calling herself Mrs Walker. What did you make of her?'

'Actually, Dick and I left for town right after I picked up the letter. We didn't get back until late afternoon, so neither of us knew anything about Peggy Browne's visit or her accident with the ladder, or about Dave Smith being in town until you told Dick when he collected you from hospital. Dick was appalled at what you told him. He knew of Dave Smith and figured that if he was involved in looking for the package and letter you could still be in danger. That's why he wanted you to get away and stay with Mum for a bit.'

18

'Getting back to the story,' George said, 'I thought my job at the base was wrapped up once I'd picked up the package and letter and I should get back to London. Dick said he planned to attend to your coffee morning the next day but would be free to drive me to Glasgow after that. We'd have lunch together and I could get an afternoon flight. I hadn't told Dick about the package and letter or my relationship to you so I just planned to keep out of sight until then and get away without you spotting me.

'When I heard the ambulance siren and saw it turn in to your driveway I assumed one of your coffee guests had collapsed. It never crossed my mind that it might be you. You've always been as fit as a fiddle, just like Mum. So imagine my shock to see you carried out on a stretcher. I rushed out, thinking you must have had a heart attack or something. You were unconscious.

'Dick guessed right away that I was somehow involved. As soon as the ambulance pulled away he beckoned me into your house, showed me the state of the kitchen and asked me what I knew about it. That's when I had to tell him you are my aunt and that I had sent the package and letter to your address but had recovered them. I have to tell you, Dick was not happy.

Anyway, after seeing your kitchen we checked the rest of the house. Every single room had been turned over in the same way. Dick agreed that whoever knocked you out and did that to your house was looking desperately for the package and letter. I'm sorry, Aunt Aggie, I made a terrible mistake sending them here. I really can't tell you how sorry I am.'

'And so you should be!' Gabriella snapped. 'Poor Aggie ended up in hospital as a result of your thoughtlessness!'

'Well Mum, we did check with the hospital to make sure she was OK. Dick called the hospital several times and when they said she could go home the next day he went to collect her.'

I sensed Gabriella's antennae quivering at 'Dick called the hospital several times'; she always did jump to conclusions. I turned away so she wouldn't see my cheeks and refocused on George's narrative.

'I did call in our reconstruction team immediately,' he was saying. 'I was hoping to get the house all cleaned up while Aunt Aggie was in hospital so she wouldn't have to see the mess in the rest of the house, but she was only in hospital the one night. The reconstruction team didn't arrive until after they released her.'

'I'm glad to hear you were so concerned,' Gabriella replied caustically.

I noticed Richard kept his face turned to the window during this exchange. Like me, he was keeping well out of it.

'Well you see, Mum,' George blundered on, 'once everything was back to normal at the base we weren't expecting anything more to happen. The break-in took me completely by surprise. You see, neither of us knew about the earlier attempts to retrieve the package and letter until Aunt Aggie told Dick about them when he picked her up from the hospital. That's when we learned that Dave Smith was involved.'

'From what Aggie told me,' Gabriella declared, taking charge as usual, 'people were looking for the package and letter almost as soon as they arrived. She had a telephone call, then a couple of students masquerading as window cleaners turned up to get them, then this Peggy Browne came to the house for them and got clobbered with a ladder for her efforts. Both those students and Peggy Browne mentioned Dave Smith's name, so he's a common factor. What you need to do now, George, is to track down this Dave Smith.'

'Now hold on, Sherlock.' George was not about to have his mother dictate his course of action. 'It's not quite as simple as that. Dave Smith is a sort of middleman in the criminal fraternity. The big boys hire him to get things done and he farms the work out keeping his own hands clean.

We know they haven't found the package and letter because I retrieved them myself, so there's a strong chance they'll come back for another look. What you and Aunt Aggie told us about those two men in York confirms the hunt is very much still on.'

George turned his attention to me.

'Dick and I are keeping watch on your house. We'll make sure it isn't invaded again. Remember to lock your door when you go out.'

'Of course I'll be locking it!' I responded tersely. 'Especially after all that's happened.'

Before Gabriella and I could comment further, Richard turned from the window. 'Tell me again, Angelina, what kind of vehicle you thought followed you to York?'

'It was a tan SUV,' I replied promptly.

'And it was a tan SUV that I saw outside the chip shop in York,' Gabriella said. 'with those two men in it, eating their fish and chips.'

'And,' I added, 'it was a tan SUV that came into the hotel car park, just before we left York and headed for home. At least I think it was tan, it was difficult to be sure of the colour in the bad lighting, but it was certainly an SUV.'

'Right, George,' Richard suddenly commanded, 'are we ready?'

'All ready, sir,' George replied smartly.

Was this my gentle neighbour telling George what to do? Most attractive!

Richard waved Gabriella and me back from

the window.

'Here they come. All in place, George?'

He responded with a thumbs up and followed Richard to one of his bedrooms that overlook my driveway. Gabriella and I tiptoed after them. We were not about to be left in the living room and miss whatever was going on. I couldn't help noticing how neat and tidy the room was, very plain and not a thing out of place. From the back of the room, where Gabriella and I were instructed most unnecessarily to stay, I could hear the SUV wheels crunch on the gravel of my driveway. Then I heard the door open and the engine grunt as it was switched off. The sounds were unusually distinct. I turned to Richard to enquire whether he had left a window open but before I could speak he put his finger to his lips. He beckoned me and Gabriella closer and whispered softly, 'We have microphones in place all round your house, Angelina. Now we watch and listen.'

19

'That's them!' Gabriella breathed, uncharacteristically careless of grammar. She grabbed my shoulder and pulled me closer to the window. 'Look, Aggie,' she whispered excitedly. 'Look at the men in sitting the front seats. Those are the two we saw in York! They are, aren't they?'

George and Richard looked questioningly at us. George pulled us gently but firmly back from the window. I nodded confirmation. 'It's definitely them.'

'Yes,' whispered Gabriella. 'We got a real shock when they came into the hotel car park.'

We watched in silence. The men seemed in no hurry to get out of their vehicle.

'Daft coming 'ere again,' one of them muttered.

It was amazing how clearly we could hear every word.

'I told 'im. She's 'id them letters somewhere. They're not in the 'ouse. We'd 'ave found 'em if they were. Stands to reason she's taken 'em with 'er. I don't know why we 'ad to come back 'ere again.'

As the two men exited slowly from their respective sides of the front of the vehicle, a third exited from the rear. I gasped. He was the man I had followed from the Bellevue Hotel to the ferry dock after taking Peggy Browne to A & E.

I turned to Richard. 'Dave Smith?' I mouthed. He nodded grimly, already tapping in numbers on his mobile phone. We heard voices again. All three men were standing in front of the vehicle.

'I don't like that back seat of yours. Felt every lump on the road. And it was covered in junk. I had to clear it before I could sit on it.'

'Aye well, Dave, that's what 'appens when you've got a girlfriend. She takes your car when she wants it. What is it today? Needed it to go for a hairdo did she? We heard you and Peg had a bit of a tiff. Playing nice are you, making it up to 'er like? Getting back into 'er good books?'

'Mind your own bloody business.'

There was a pause, then Dave reasserted his authority. 'Right you two, let's try and do it the easy way this time. Ring the doorbell one of you, and see if she's in. Then leave me to do the talking if she is.'

'You can ring t'doorbell yourself! But I can tell yer she won't be in. She's in York. Yer didn't know that, did yer?'

Dave looked startled. 'Don't be so daft,' he said scathingly. 'What makes you think she's in York?'

'We saw 'er there, didn't we, Mick?' replied the taller of the two men.

'Aye, me and Ron saw 'er there,' the shorter man confirmed.

'Don't give me that!' Dave spat at them. 'When were you two buggers ever in York? I bet you don't even know where York is.'

Ron didn't like that. He glared at Dave and bunched a fist. 'Course we know where York is. That's where we're from. We went to York this last weekend, didn't we Mick?'

'Aye,' Mick replied. 'We did an' all. We went to York. It were our Mam's birthday. She were 'aving a party, like. We allus go down to York for our Mam's birthday. The 'ole family go. Sixty-three she were. She 'ad a cake with sixty-three candles on it, didn't she, Ron?'

'Aye, she did,' replied his brother, mellow in contrast to his former belligerence. 'And who was the daft bugger that tried to light all sixty-three of 'em at once? Nearly set the 'ouse on fire, 'e did, Dave. It were a good thing our Mam 'ad the teapot 'andy to dowse it. That could 'ave ruined the cake, all that tea on it.'

'It were all right though, weren't it,' Mick countered. 'Bit like a trifle but it were all right, everyone said so. And our Mam said she'd save the candles that didn't get lit for next year.'

Dave had clearly heard enough homely exchange between the two men we now knew to be brothers, Ron and Mick. 'To hell with your

Mother's cake. Get on and ring that doorbell like I told you.'

Ron stood his ground. 'She won't be 'ere, I tell you, Dave. Me and Mick saw 'er three times in York while we were there, and she were still there last night.'

Dave hesitated. 'When did you see her, then? Was she invited to your Mother's party?'

Ron bunched his fist again. Dave backed away.

'Anyway,' he continued, regaining ground, 'how do you know it was her that you saw?'

'Our Mick 'as a good memory for faces.' Ron chose to ignore the gibe about his mother's party but his fists were half way to re-clenching. 'You tell 'im about it Mick, 'ow you recognised 'er.'

'Aye well,' said Mick, shaking his head modestly, 'I remembered what she looked like from when we first came to the 'ouse wearing them police caps that you gave us.'

He looked at his brother angrily. 'It were our Ron as knocked 'er out. It were a bloody daft thing to do because then we couldn't ask 'er where the bloody letters were. We 'ad to search the 'ole 'ouse and we still couldn't find them. 'E must 'ave 'it 'er bloody hard because she were still lying on the floor, out cold when we left the 'ouse. I tell yer, I were bloody relieved to see 'er walking around in York. That could 'ave been nasty.'

'She was still breathing when we left the 'ouse though.' Ron said righteously.

'Never mind all that!' Dave was getting impatient. 'If you saw her in York, why didn't you get the package and letter from her right then?'

'We tried, didn't we, Ron?' Mick continued. 'We were in the car when we first saw 'er. She was walking along t'road towards t'river. We saw 'er turn and go down t'steps that go to t'river bank. We could see that she were only carrying a small bag slung across 'er shoulder so Ron and me thought she wouldn't be carrying the package and letter with 'er. We figured she must 'ave left them somewhere. So we parked the car and watched for 'er to come back so we could follow 'er. I'll say this for 'er, she must be a bloody good walker. We 'ad to wait nearly three hours for 'er to get back.'

Mick paused and smiled at his audience of two, presumably looking for appreciation. 'Get on with it,' Dave snarled.

'Well,' Mick obliged, 'then we followed 'er to this 'otel by the river. Nice place it was. There were other people going in so we followed behind them, 'idden like. Then we saw 'er join a line of people waiting to go into the restaurant that was inside the 'otel. Then we 'ad a bit of luck. Someone must 'ave said something to 'er because we 'eard 'er say that she allus stays at this 'otel when she comes to York and she 'ad a lovely view of the river from 'er room on the third floor. Ron and me didn't need telling twice. We went up the stairs to the third floor like a flash.'

Ron nodded confirmation.

Mick continued his saga. 'When we got up onto the third floor we could tell that there were only two rooms on the landing that would look out on the river so it 'ad to be one of them. Then a man and 'is wife came out of one of the two rooms so she 'ad to be in the other. Then we 'ad a bit of luck. We saw a maid and told 'er our pass key wasn't working so she let us in and we told 'er we'd get another when we went downstairs again.'

'So what did you find there?' Dave was getting impatient but Mick was in no hurry to finish his story.

' I tell you, Dave, we looked everywhere in that room but we didn't find anything. We thought they would be in 'er luggage but she 'adn't brought any luggage so there were nothing for us to look in. We knew she'd been in the room though because there was a mucky cup and a used tea bag on a tray by the window.'

'And the greedy bitch 'ad eaten all the biscuits.' Ron added. 'She'd left the empty wrappers on the tray. Shortbread they were an' all.'

'We did search the room,' Mick insisted, 'but there was nothing there.'

'You stupid buggers!' Dave snapped. 'She must have left her luggage in her car. Why didn't you look in her car?'

"Ow were we to know what 'er car looked like?' Ron was all injured innocence.

'You told me you looked in her car when you searched the house.'

'Oh aye, we looked in 'er car all right but we didn't look at the outside.'

'She might 'ave gone to York by train and not by car at all.' added Mick.

These two were a real duet!

Dave Smith's body language indicated he had had enough. He marched to my front door and rang the bell. He tried a second and a third time, then getting no response tried the handle. Thank goodness George had locked the door.

'Told yer!' Ron shouted triumphantly.

'You stupid buggers!' Dave was shouting too now, heedless of alerting the neighbourhood. 'Get yourselves round the house and see if you can find another way in.'

Mick shrugged and ambled off down the far side the house. Ron stood his ground for a minute, fists clenching and unclenching, then went in the other direction. I thought we might lose their scintillating conversation when they disappeared, leaving Dave Smith to fume at the front of the house. There was in fact silence for a few minutes, presumably while the brothers investigated. Then we heard their voices again, coming from the back of the house. George must have done a very good job with his microphones.

'Yer know Ron I don't like Dave's attitude, calling us stupid buggers. We were the ones that searched 'er 'ouse and we were the ones that saw 'er in York and followed 'er to 'er 'otel and searched 'er room. That were initiative, that were.

If it weren't for us 'e wouldn't even know she went to York.'

'No, and 'ow were we to know if she went in a car and if she left 'er luggage in it? Second sight, that's what 'e expects us to 'ave, second sight. We do all the work and 'e just sits around giving orders. And 'e 'asn't paid us yet for doing the 'ouse over.'

'Well I say we don't do any more for 'im until 'e pays us for what we've done already.'

'Aye. And I reckon 'e should pay us for what we did in York an' all.'

'I've been thinking about that.'

'What, paying us for York?'

'No, 'er car, like. It were in 'er garage. It were a Beetle. Don't you remember, it were a bit old but it were a Beetle.'

'Oh yeah. I'd forgotten that.'

'Well, we told Dave we didn't know 'ow she got to York, but I remember now, there were a mucky old Beetle in that 'otel car park, a blue one.'

'I don't remember seeing it and we looked all round for 'er car.'

'Aye, but it were getting dark and we were looking for something more classy. You said she'd be driving a classy car. '

'It might not 'ave been 'ers. Anyway, we won't mention it to Dave.'

There was silence again for a while, then we heard Dave Smith bellow, 'Have you two buggers gone to sleep? Where are you? Get back here.'

We heard the crunch of feet on gravel as Ron and Mick returned to the front of the house.

'What the hell have you two been doing back there. You've had time to check round the house six times over.'

'We've been thinking, Dave.'

'Thinking! That's a laugh! With what?'

'No Dave,' Ron stretched up to his full height, almost a head taller than Dave Smith. 'We were talking about money. Our money. The money you owe us.'

'Don't be daft. I don't owe you anything until you bring me those bloody letters.'

'That wasn't what we agreed, Dave. You said you'd pay us 'alf for searching the 'ouse and 'alf for finding the letters. That were what we agreed.'

'Now don't worry lads, you'll be paid. You know me. You'll be paid in full when you come up with the goods.'

'No Dave, like I told yer, she's in York and we're not going all the way to York again. You can go to York yourself if you want to. Just 'and over t'money that we're owed for searching t'ouse and we'll call it quits.'

'I haven't got the money. I haven't been paid myself yet. I'll pay you when I get paid.'

'No, you'll pay us now.' Ron had moved closer to Dave and was towering menacingly over him. Dave stepped back.

'Hey, hold on guys, you know you'll get

your money.'

'Damn right!' growled Mick, closing up on him, fists clenched.

I had to marvel at the way that the Ron and Mick who had reminisced so happily about their Mother's birthday party could morph so quickly into thugs. Ron put his hands firmly round Dave's throat while Mick went systematically through his pockets.

'There's nowt 'ere but two tens and a fiver. No bank cards. Did they cancel yer cards, Dave? Not been paying yer bills then? Dear, dear.'

'Believe me, guys,' he wailed, 'you'll get your money. I just don't have it on me.'

Ron signalled to his brother and pointed to the SUV. 'Come on. Just leave 'im. We can catch up with 'im later. He's not worth doing time for. Let's go.'

Ron hurled Dave to the ground and hurried after his brother who was already climbing into the driving seat of the SUV. Mick started the engine.

'Hey, wait for me lads!' Dave was getting up from the ground.

Ron leaned out of the passenger window. 'Can't 'ear what you say, Dave.'

'Wait!'

'What did you say, Dave?' the SUV was beginning to move up the drive towards the gate.

'You stupid buggers!'

'That's us, Dave, stupid buggers.' Mick

waved the notes he had retrieved from Dave Smith's wallet.

' 'Ope you've got some money for the bus, Dave.'

The SUV turned out of the gateway into the waiting police block.

20

That should have been the end of the story. George, Richard, Gabriella and I were standing by the window in Richard's living room. He'd produced a bottle of malt whiskey and glasses and we were happily toasting a successful operation. I thanked Richard sincerely for all his help and told him that that despite everything I wouldn't have missed the excitement of the last week for words. I assured him that I had no lingering ill-effects from my head injury and that I considered getting a completely refurbished house to be more than enough compensation for the trouble George's investigation had caused. It must have been the whisky making me mellow because I even smiled at George.

Gabriella, on the other hand, was patently glowing with pride in what she regarded as indisputable evidence of her son's aptitude and genius. She took his arm as she stood and watched the waves of incoming tide roll up, the swooping seagulls and the ducks and oystercatchers down by the water. She sighed with satisfaction.

'You're so lucky to live in a spot like this,

Aggie,' she declared, 'looking out of your window every day on all this, the sea and the hills, the ferries, fishing boats and cargo ships and the cruise ships and submarines. I could never get tired of it.'

Before I could remind her that there was nothing to stop her moving here if she chose to do so, she turned to Richard and simpered – that's the only word to describe it, she actually simpered – 'I'm sure you enjoy living here too, er, Richard, or would you prefer me to call you Dick?'

I was aghast, although I really shouldn't have been surprised.

I looked quickly at Richard, hoping she hadn't embarrassed him too much. My sympathy was wasted though. Without missing a beat and looking rather pleased, if a little pink, he waved his glass as if to toast her.

'Angelina calls me Richard,' he replied happily. 'And yes, I do enjoy living here. We're away from the city bustle and congestion, but we still have easy access to the rest of the world. What's not to like? My house suits me very well and I have exceptionally good neighbours.'

He looked meaningfully at me as he said this.

I felt a frisson. Goodness gracious! Was Richard flirting with me now, or was he just trying to discourage Gabriella without hurting her feelings? One way or the other, she got the message. I'll say this for her, she always was quick on the uptake.

'Then,' she replied smoothly, 'I'll call you Richard too, just as you call Aggie Angelina.'

She turned quickly back to the window to hide her feelings as she spoke. I felt almost sorry for her. After all, she is my sister and Richard is rather good-looking. Maybe it was because she was looking so intently out of the window to hide her embarrassment that Gabriella's gaze suddenly fixed on something along the road that runs between our houses and the shore.

'Just a minute!' She pointed to a lone figure standing at the bus stop.

'Look, down there, look Aggie, isn't that Dave Smith? He's just too far away to be absolutely sure but I think it's him.'

Richard produced binoculars from behind the curtain like a rabbit out of a hat.

'Here you are, Gabriella,' he said gallantly, 'have a look with these. I keep my binocs handy for birds and ships. Maybe you can spot a Dave Smith with them.'

Teasing or flirting back? Hmm ...

Gabriella was not to be put off, though. She fiddled with the focus until she could see clearly, and peered intently at the bus stop.

'I knew I was right,' she said, shaking her head and passing the binoculars to her son. 'Here, George, you take a look. See if you think it's Dave Smith.'

George put down his whiskey glass on the window sill. He took the binoculars, refocused, and trained them on the bus stop. He nodded.

'You know, Dick, Mum's right. Take a look. See what you think.'

He passed the binoculars to Richard, who focused on the lone figure at the bus stop for a minute, then put them down.

'Well spotted, Gabriella. Yes it's Dave Smith, all right. He wasn't in the SUV with them. They were going to drive off without him. I bet he slipped down the side of the house and climbed over the wall onto the road while the police were busy talking to Ron and Mick.'

'Well, what shall we do now?' Gabriella was ready for action. 'Shall we call the police and tell them Dave's there at the bus stop?'

'No, Mum,' George told her. 'There's nothing to charge any of them with. The reason Dick and I set up this surveillance on Aunt Aggie's house was to see when it would be safe for her to come home. You see, until now, we weren't sure whether the search was still on for the package and letter.'

'Well,' retorted Gabriella, 'obviously the search is still on and it isn't safe, so why did the police just talk to them and go away? Why didn't they take them and lock them up?'

'They would have invented legitimate reasons for being here today. Dick called the police and reported a suspicious vehicle in Aunt Aggie's driveway to make them think twice before coming again. So we'll just let Dave Smith get on the bus and go on his way for now. I know it seems a bit of an anticlimax but there it is.'

Gabriella was disappointed. 'But George, we overheard their conversation. Didn't you record it for evidence? Those men, Ron and Mick, admitted to breaking into the house and to attacking your aunt, and even to seeing her again in York. And it was clear from their conversation that it was Dave who was paying them to do it. Surely that's enough to implicate them all?'

George didn't say anything, just looked at his mother gently and shook his head. The penny finally dropped.

'Oh, of course! You spooks don't want to expose your part in it.'

I was feeling a bit left out of all the discussion. Merciful heavens, I might as well not have been in the room. After all, I had been the victim. I was the one whose life had been impacted, whose house had been wrecked. I was the one who ended up in hospital and who might still be in danger. Yet I was the only one who hadn't even been invited to have a look through the binoculars. Well, that was easily taken care of. I picked up the now discarded binoculars to see for myself.

I focused down onto the road below. Yes, there was no question. It was Dave Smith all right. As I watched, a car pulled up alongside the bus stop. The kerb-side door opened and Dave Smith got in. Now what? I trained the binoculars on the driver. Powerful as the binoculars were though, I was unable to see the driver's face because it was hidden behind the window frame and the roof of the car. I had the impression though that the driver was wearing something light brown, possibly military fatigues.

'Quickly,' I signalled to the others, 'Dave's getting into a car.' I pointed down to the bus stop as I passed the binoculars to George.

'Did you get the car number?' George asked as he watched the car drive away.

'I tried,' I said. 'But it was unreadable, must have had mud on it.'

'Yes,' he said thoughtfully, 'I couldn't make it out either. I was too late. The car was a black Vauxhall Astra, but that doesn't mean much because there are lots of those around here.'

'The driver might be wearing a uniform,' I suggested.

'Uniform? You thought he was wearing a uniform?'

'I can't be positive but I think he could have been wearing that sort of military cotton camouflage uniform, you know, all beiges and browns. But it might just have been shadows on beige clothing. I can't even be sure it was a man driving the car. I suppose it could just as easily have been a woman, maybe Peggy Browne. Don't you remember Ron and Mick joking about Peggy having Dave Smith's car today?'

'Quite possible.' Richard now joined in the speculation.

'She did have his car, according to Ron and Mick,' I repeated. 'And she could have been wearing, say, brown trousers and a tan jacket. I only saw the driver's clothes for a second. It was the colours that made me think of military fatigues. I probably wouldn't even have made that connection if George hadn't been telling us about his investigation at the base.'

'When you came out of hospital, Angelina,' Richard said thoughtfully, 'didn't you tell me you saw a man get into a black car, and that you followed him to the car ferry?'

'Yes, and it turned out to be Dave Smith. He was driving a black Vauxhall that day. I couldn't swear it was the same car today though, because I was focused on the people, not the car. It was George that said it was a Vauxhall today.'

'Well, there's nothing more to be done now except maintain surveillance on your house, Angelina, although I doubt your visitors will be back today after the police showed up. You weren't supposed to be back yet, but it's good to see you.'

'And it's good to be back,' I told him. 'Look Richard, Gabriella and I need to go home now and settle in. Why don't you and George come round later for dinner. It'll have to be a takeaway but we have choices. Fish and chips, Indian, Chinese, Italian or a frozen pizza from the store.'

'I vote for Indian,' proclaimed Gabriella. So Indian it was.

21

A few days later, life having settled down again, I was checking my calendar and discovered a 10 a.m. dental appointment. I'd forgotten about it in the whirl of the past week. I mentioned this to Gabriella, who was playing card games on my laptop, and asked if she wanted to go with me, stressing that I would need to leave in fifteen minutes.

'Just give me a few minutes to get ready,' she said. 'I'll go and have a mooch round the high street while you're having your teeth done.'

Now I know my sister. She can take ages getting ready to go out, so I said again, 'You'll have to hurry, Gabs. I really do have to leave in fifteen minutes. If you're not in the car by then, I'll just have to leave without you.'

It was a lovely day, so with those fifteen minutes to spare I went out into the garden patch by my front door to replenish the bird feeder. Then, keeping a careful eye on the time, I wandered down the far side of the house to pull some weeds I spotted growing among a patch of heathers.

To be sure Gabriella was ready to go, I went

back into the house just before the fifteen-minute deadline. She wasn't waiting for me in the kitchen as I had hoped. I peeked into her bedroom. She wasn't there either, nor was she in the bathroom.

Then I heard her voice from the living room. She was speaking heatedly to someone.

'I tell you, you've got the wrong person. You need to talk to my sister. She's the one who lives here. I'm just visiting. Believe me, I've no idea what you're talking about.'

'Cut the crap lady,' came a gruff male snarl. 'Where are they?'

'Look, I've already told you, I honestly don't know what you're talking about. You'll have to ask my sister.'

I held my breath. There was a short silence, then, 'Look lady, we don't want to 'urt you again, so you'd best tell us where you've 'idden 'em. We know you've got 'em somewhere.'

The voice belonged to either Ron or Mick, and the 'we' must mean they were both in there with Gabriella. It was my fault. I'd left the front door unlocked when I went out to the garden and they had simply walked in. They had mistaken Gabriella for me and now she was being threatened with bodily harm because of my carelessness. I had to act quickly before she ended up in hospital just as I had done.

I banged hard on the living room door and shouted at the top of my voice,

'Gabs! Come on, hurry up! I have to go.

Where are you? Come on, we're going to be late!'

Then I turned tail and raced through the kitchen into the garage, leaving the kitchen door open behind me so they would see which way I went. My thought was to lure them away from Gabriella and call Richard for help.

I pressed the garage door opener button on the wall, scrambled into my blue Beetle and locked the doors. The key was already in the ignition ready to leave for the dentist. As I put my hand on the key, the kitchen door flew open and an irate Ron leaped at the car and tugged at the door handle. I put my hand on the horn and kept it there.

Mick came rushing into the garage to join his brother, ran round the car and tugged at the door handle on the other side. They were both shouting but their words were drowned out by the horn. Probably just as well. Then they saw me through the car windows. They both stopped shouting and stared. I kept my hand on the horn. The noise did it. They turned tail and fled out of the garage and up the driveway. I stayed in the car with my hand still firmly on the horn.

As I watched Ron and Micks' exodus up the driveway Gabriella appeared at the kitchen door. I unlocked the car door for her to get in. She flung open the door and yelled over the horn blast,

'For goodness sake Aggie stop that racket! They've gone!'

'Have they?' I took my hand off the horn.

'Better get in the car and wait until we're really sure. Don't forget, they've already attacked me once.'

But my impulsive sister was not about to wait. She took off on foot up the drive. I got out of the car and followed more cautiously.

'Quick, Aggie, come and see,' she gloated as I caught her up. 'They won't be able to wriggle out of it this time. Just look!'

I followed her the rest of the way up the drive to the road and looked. Parked just along from the house was a tan SUV. Standing facing the SUV with their backs towards us, wrists handcuffed behind them were Ron and Mick. We watched as they were led into a police van parked behind the SUV.

'All's well that ends well, Angelina.' Richard was standing beside me. I resisted a strong urge to throw myself at him and hug him.

'Did you call the police?'

'Yes I did. When I saw Ron and Mick arrive I alerted the police right away. You'd think that being questioned the other day would have been enough to deter them from coming back. But I wasn't really worried because I knew they wouldn't to get into the house now that you're keeping your door locked. By the way, what was the car horn all about? It certainly had them racing back up the drive. I hope you weren't taking any risks.'

'Oh, Aggie didn't take any risks,' Gabriella

chimed in peevishly. 'She was safe outside in the garden. I was the one that nearly got murdered!'

Richard looked bewildered.

'She's right,' I said. I turned to Gabriella.

'I'm really sorry, Gabs. It was entirely my fault. I'm afraid I did leave the door unlocked when I went out to fill up the bird feeder. Then I got side-tracked by some weeds down the far side of the house that needed pulling.'

To forestall further indignation from my sister I turned back to Richard.

'We were very lucky you saw those guys and called the police. We're very, very grateful.'

He smiled happily. 'Ah well, I can't take all the credit. I did have warning. When George dismantled the surveillance system around your house he left the monitors on your driveway in place so I could check on any visitors. It's a good thing he did and fortunately no harm was done.'

Gabriella was aghast.

'No harm!' she screeched. 'No harm! I was in the house alone when those two thugs came in. I was almost killed! If you saw them go into the house, Richard, why did you just stand there watching? Why didn't you come in after them?'

'I'm sorry Gabriella, I wasn't really worried at the time you see, because I knew Angelina was safe in the garden. I didn't occur to me that you might still be indoors.'

That really inflamed my sister. She always did have a short fuse. Her reaction was to launch into an unnecessarily detailed account of how she had specifically closed the living room door to prevent a draught round her ankles. That was an exaggeration right there of course. There are no draughts in my house. She went on to tell us that when she heard the living room door open, she hadn't looked up right away because she assumed it was me, coming to remind her, quite needlessly, that time was getting on. She knew very well that there was still plenty of time before we had to leave for my dental appointment. The next thing she knew, Ron and Mick were standing over her.

'Menacingly,' she added. 'They demanded to know what I had done with that package and a letter that weren't for me and I had no right to keep.'

'Of course,' she said, glaring at me, 'they thought I was you. But if you were outside the house, Aggie, why didn't you see them and why didn't they see you?'

'They must have come while I was weeding down the side. I didn't see them and I didn't hear them either.'

Gabriella looked at Richard and smirked as though she had scored a point. There are times when I feel quite negative towards my sister.

'There's been a lot of traffic this morning,' I asserted before she could suggest a hearing test.

Richard intervened. 'I'm sorry, Gabriella. I called the police as soon as I saw the two of them go down Angelina's driveway. The reason I wasn't worried at first was because I assumed the door was locked. Then when I saw them go into the house my only concern was that they might damage it again. I knew Angelina was outside and I'm afraid I forgot for the moment that you might be inside.'

'So where did you think I was?' she flashed back at him.

Richard wisely ignored her question and continued, 'When I saw Angelina go back into the house, knowing those two had gone inside I rushed over. But just as I reached the front door the garage door opened and the car horn started blaring. The next thing, Ron and Mick rushed out of the garage looking terrified. Then the horn stopped and the two of you came out and went up the driveway and I followed you. I think we may have seen the last of those two thugs this time, but unless you've any objection, Angelina, I'll keep up the surveillance on your driveway a bit longer.'

'No objection whatever, In fact I'd prefer you to keep it up.'

'Well I'm going to text George about this!' Gabriella was still not happy. 'He had no right to leave while we were still in danger.'

'But Gabs,' I said, attempting to soothe her, 'Richard is here and George's surveillance system is still on the driveway. It worked this morning, and Ron and Mick have been taken off by the police. We've nothing to worry about now. Come on, let's go indoors.'

Gabriella shrugged. She was still not convinced but turned back towards the house with us. Then we heard a vehicle screech to a halt on the road outside. I went back to the gate to see what was happening.

'Quick, come and see!' I called to the others. 'You're not going to believe this. Look who just got out of that black car. I do believe she's going to get into Ron and Mick's SUV.'

The three of us watched the back of Peggy Browne disappearing into the tan SUV. She executed a neat three-point turn and followed a black sedan down the road.

'Time for coffee,' I said weakly. 'Would you like to join us, Richard?'

The three of us trooped into my kitchen. I felt the occasion called for more than my usual instant coffee. I ground some beans and loaded my little-used coffee maker.

The telephone rang. 'Dr Maud, this is the dental office calling. You missed your appointment.'

22

After lunch Gabriella told me she was going back home to Bungay.

'I've already checked trains on the web,' she said. 'It's too late to set off today so I'll have to go tomorrow. What's the best way to get to the station in Glasgow from here? Doesn't your bus take me there, you know, the one that goes over the ferry?'

I was puzzled. I was under the impression she'd been thoroughly enjoying her visit. Had something gone wrong in Bungay? I hadn't been aware of any urgent phone calls.

'Yes, the bus will take you to the either station in Glasgow,' I said. 'Or I could run you there in the car. But Gabs, you've only just arrived. Why go back so soon? Has something happened in Bungay?'

'No,' she said quietly, 'I've just realised it's time for me to go home.'

This was most unlike my sister. Something was troubling her. I sat down at the table beside her.

'I was expecting you to stay at least a fortnight as you usually do,' I said carefully. 'If there's nothing to rush back to Bungay for, something must be bothering you here. Have I upset you in some way?'

Gabriella didn't reply immediately. She got up from the table then sat down again. She put her elbows on the table, both thumbs in her mouth and moved her lower teeth from side to side across her thumb nails. She has done this when upset ever since we were children,. By this time I could guess what was bothering her but it surely wasn't enough to warrant rushing away tomorrow.

'No,' she said eventually. 'It's not you. Of course it's not you. You haven't upset me at all. In fact I've been having the best time ever these last few days. It's just that ... '

'Come on, tell me what's wrong.'

'Well, it's just that ... it's just that I feel superfluous.'

Oh dear, I was right. Richard was her problem. Gabriella had made no secret of her attraction to him but I hadn't thought it amounted to anything more than mild flirtation on her part. For his part, Richard didn't seem to notice or indeed didn't appear to mind if he did notice. I was very glad of this, but this was not the time to say so.

'Of course you're not superfluous. You know very well I couldn't have done without you these last few days.'

That was true. I put my arm round her shoulders.

'Come on, let's talk about it and we'll sort it all out as we always do. Why do you feel superfluous?'

Gabriella blushed. This was unusual; it takes a lot to get her to blush.

'All right,' she said. 'I'd better tell you. You never did see things right under your nose. You've probably been too wrapped up in this fake letter business of George's to notice. Anyway, Aggie, that neighbour of yours is a very attractive man.'

'Well yes, he is nice looking,' I allowed cautiously. 'And a very nice person too. He's thoughtful, he gets on well with everybody here and I think he's probably quite intelligent. One of the nurses at the hospital said he was quite a dish.'

'And?'

'And what?'

'I know you find him attractive too, although you try not to show it. I also know I do, but unfortunately he only has eyes for you. Just like the song, in fact. I've tried to engage his attention several times but he somehow always manages to keep his distance. Slippery as an eel he is with me! He's different with you though.'

Was it that obvious? It was still early days for Richard and me.

'Gabs,' I said firmly, 'you're just letting your imagination run away with you. Richard's a lovely man, a wonderful, caring friend. I couldn't wish for a better neighbour but that's as far as it goes. He lives his life next door and I live mine right here. You've nothing to be jealous about.'

That was true. Well, so far at any rate. Hopefully not for ever.

'Jealous!' she snorted. 'What makes you think I'm jealous? You've just said there's nothing going between the two of you. There's nothing to be jealous about.'

I was relieved to see that she seemed to be taking control again. The last thing I wanted to do was to make her unhappy. I made a mental note to avoid contact with Richard for the remainder of her visit. I had an idea that should help.

'I do hope you'll reconsider and stay on here for another week or two,' I said. 'Please do. I want to take you to a brand new garden centre that's opened. They have a fantastic range of trees, plants and shrubs, all suitable for our climate. You'll love it. Seriously, you'd be sorry to miss it. And there's a new restaurant right next door. If we go to the garden centre tomorrow we could have lunch there.'

I had said the magic words. Gabriella went straight to my laptop computer and opened the lid.

'What did you say it's called? I'll see if it has a web page. Yes let's do the garden centre. I'm sure there won't be any more cloak and dagger stuff while I'm here.'

She was quite wrong.

23

I knew that Gabriella of the green thumbs would want to take her time in the garden centre. We set off early so as to arrive as soon as they opened, when there would be fewer other customers and she could mooch round unimpeded. This proved an excellent plan because we were the only people to go into the bedding plant section when we arrived, a.k.a. Aladdin's Cave to Gabriella. She was only on the second row of plants when I was ready to move on. I needed a few geraniums so I suggested she select some for me while I went to check out the lunch menu at the restaurant next door. Gabriella was delighted to be asked to choose for me. She always did have a poor opinion of my horticultural skills, quite unwarranted of course.

Like the garden centre, the restaurant had only just opened. There was a delicious aroma of coffee brewing and a tempting array of cakes and pastries in the glass case below the counter. Quite irresistible! I went straight back to Gabriella to suggest that we go and enjoy a coffee while all is quiet at the restaurant. I found her still in the bedding plant section, deep in conversation with another customer, an older woman. Rather than interrupt a conversation she was so obviously enjoying, I went to look at the shrub section, leaving my sister and her new friend to converse among the bedding plants. After all, there was no immediate urgency for coffee.

I took my time looking at the shrubs, then went to look at the trees. Gabriella still hadn't come to join me so I assumed she was still occupied in the bedding plant section. I decided to go and browse the gift shop before going to see how the geranium selection was progressing.

The gift shop at the garden centre had large picture windows overlooking the car park. Looking out, I could see a number of cars arriving. I looked fondly out on my little blue Beetle sandwiched between a Land Rover and a black car, and congratulated myself on coming early, thereby securing a parking spot close to the door. Then I noticed two women walking across the car park towards the cars. Peering more closely I could see that one was Gabriella balancing a large tray of geraniums and the other was the grey-haired woman I had seen her talking to inside the garden centre. There was something familiar about the other woman, but I just couldn't place her. It didn't seem important at the time. More importantly, I knew that Gabriella would need help getting the geraniums into the car. She had my spare car key to unlock the doors, but the lock on the car bonnet can be very tricky. In fact the plants might be better on the back seat. I hurried out to go and help her, pulling my own car key out of my pocket as I went.

I was in for a shock when I reached the car park. There was no sign of Gabriella or the other woman. Six geranium plants in their plastic pots lay strewn on the ground alongside my blue Beetle, right next to an empty space where the black car had been parked. The green Land Rover remained parked on the other side but there was no one in it and no other people around to witness what had happened. Despite my decision to avoid contact with Richard while Gabriella was still staying with me, I called him on my mobile.

'Did you get the number of the black car?' Richard asked the obvious question.

'No,' I told him. 'There was no reason to look at the black car until after it had gone.'

'What about the woman your sister was talking to? Did you get a good look at her?'

'Not really, I didn't pay much attention when I first saw her talking to Gabriella in among the bedding plants, just an older woman with grey hair, wearing a dark coat over a long skirt. When she was walking towards the cars I only saw her back view. I did think at the time that she looked vaguely familiar but wasn't concerned. Gabriella was balancing the tray of geraniums and the other woman was just walking along with her. But Richard, I have an awful suspicion. Could that woman have been Peggy Browne wearing a grey wig?'

'Wouldn't your sister have suspected it was Peggy Browne? She seems pretty astute.'

'I doubt it. Gabriella never saw her close up. The other day when I saw Peggy climbing into Ron and Mick's SUV, Gabriella was still busy telling you what had happened with them inside the house. By the time you and she came to the gate, Peggy was practically inside the SUV and driving off.'

'Right, let's assume the woman you saw was her. We don't know how, but somehow she managed to persuade your sister to get into her own car. She doesn't know of course that you have a twin sister, so just as Ron and Mick did the other day, she'll assume she's talking to you. My guess is she'll be headed either to Glasgow to meet up with Dave Smith or, more likely, she's driving straight back to your house on the assumption that the package and letter are still there and intends to make you give them to her.

'I'm going to make a couple of calls right away. They can't have got far. I'll try to have them intercepted. In the meantime I want you to get in your car, lock the door, and wait there until the police arrive. Leave everything as it is on the ground for the police to see. Don't move the plants. You'll need to give a statement too, your account of what happened. This is serious, Angelina. I'm going to stay right here in case my guess is right and they turn up at your house.' He rang off.

Now I don't like other people telling me

what to do but it seemed a good plan, so I watched the empty space next to me, ready to leap out and wave my arms to prevent another car from driving into it but no other car came to claim it.

I was surprised how soon a police car arrived. I got out of my car.

'Dr Angelina Maud? We're here to investigate a report that a woman has been abducted from this car park.'

'Yes. Thank you for coming so quickly.'

'We were in the area, ma'am. We got a call on the radio.'

The policeman looked at the geraniums on the ground beside the empty parking slot.

'This is where it happened?'

'Yes.'

'You saw it happen?'

'I was in the gift shop in the garden centre. I happened to look out of the window and saw my sister carrying these plants to the car,' I pointed to the geraniums on the ground, 'There was another woman walking with her. I came out to help her load them into my car but when I got here, they'd all gone, my sister, the other woman and the car that had been parked in this slot next to mine.'

'Your sister?'

'My twin sister.'

'You look alike?'

'We're identical twins.'

'Which is your car, ma'am?'

'This one,' I indicated my blue Beetle. It

seemed a superfluous question because I'd been sitting in it when he arrived.

'And you haven't moved your car since this happened?'

'No.'

'And you're sure there was another car parked here next to you?'

'Oh yes. And I watched to see no one else parked here until you arrived.'

'Can you describe the car that you say was parked here? Colour? Make? Registration number?'

'I can only tell you that it was a black sedan. Nothing special about it.'

'Right, we'll take some pictures and you'll need to come in to the police station and give us a statement. Do you happen to have a photograph of your sister with you, in your wallet maybe?'

'No, but she looks just like me. I told you, we're identical twins. Oh, and she's wearing a red pea jacket, beige trousers and tan suede shoes.'

'OK, take a photo of her to the station when you go to give your statement.'

'Does that mean that I can go home now?'

'Yes, but if it's OK with you, I'll take a picture of you for now since you tell me you look the same as your sister but don't forget to bring that proper photo of her to the station. Drive home carefully.'

I thanked him again and was about to get into my car when the owner of the green Land

Rover parked the other side of me arrived, carrying a red rhododendron. A small boy, maybe seven or eight years old, tagged along.

The policeman greeted him. 'Good morning, sir. I wonder if you could help me.'

'I will if I can. What's up?'

'When you parked here, did you notice what other cars were parked in this area?'

'Sorry, I was one of the first to arrive. The car park was pretty empty. Other cars were arriving but I can't tell you anything about them. I just went straight into the garden centre.'

'I was watching them, Dad.'

Everyone looked at the small boy.

'I know what cars came in after us. I was watching to see what they were.'

The policeman looked at the father, who nodded.

'Aye, knows his cars does our Michael. Don't you son?'

This was the small boy's moment. 'I can tell you the cars that came in after us. First there was this battered old blue Beetle and this lady.' He pointed to me. 'She got out with another lady that looked just like her except they were wearing different clothes. Then a black Vauxhall Astra came and parked next to the Beetle and another old lady got out of that car. Then you made me go with you into that stupid garden centre, Dad.'

24

I agonised about Gabriella all the way home. I felt so guilty about clearing off and leaving her by herself among the bedding plants in the garden centre. How could I have been so selfish? It really wouldn't have hurt me to stay there and look at plants with her. After all, she was picking over the plants for my benefit, at my request. If she hadn't been there alone, Peggy Browne might never have approached her. If only I hadn't gone to the restaurant when I did, I might have seen Peggy Browne go into the bedding plant area and might have recognised her despite the silver hair. So many 'ifs' and 'might haves', and all my fault! Hindsight, they say is twenty-twenty.

I didn't want to think about what Peggy Browne might have done to get Gabriella into her car. It was completely out of character for my sister to go off with a stranger, and leave without telling me. Even if she had somehow been persuaded to get into the other woman's car, she would never have left her precious plants behind in the car park. No, I just couldn't see her getting into that car willingly, but how? Could she have been drugged? Could she have been clobbered on the head as I had been? Would she too end up in hospital? Oh my poor sister! Tears streamed down my face as I drove home.

Imagine my shock therefore when I got home and found Gabriella in my living room chatting happily and sipping white wine with Richard. I was absolutely gobsmacked! My mind did not focus immediately on the fact that she was home, safe and apparently unaffected by being kidnapped in a garden centre car park. That old song, 'Cocktails for two' came into my mind. They weren't sipping cocktails though. I could see the label on the bottle, standing inelegantly on a magazine on the table, presumably to be handy for refills. It was the bottle of wine I had put by for dinner that evening. I couldn't believe it! My sister never did have any qualms about helping herself to my possessions. She hadn't even had the decency to put a third glass on the table ready for my return! I had been worried sick since her disappearance from the garden centre car park, dreading that she might have been killed, and had been beating myself up thinking how I should have appreciated her more and been a better sister to her, and here she was, chirpy as a cricket, drinking my wine and flirting with my neighbour! Yes, flirting! I was too dumbfounded say anything. Furthermore, Gabriella didn't look overly pleased to see me. The vixen!

Well, I have never been a gooseberry and

didn't intend to be one then! Let her try to hook Richard if she could. Good luck to her! He was nothing to me. I marched straight to the kitchen and put the kettle on for a cup of tea.

I was too wrapped up in my indignation to notice Richard follow me into the kitchen until he spoke.

'Maybe you could make tea for all three of us, Angelina.'

'All right. I can do that,' I replied, more sharply that I intended.

Richard's voice was gentle, soothing. Concerned? Maybe.

'I'm very glad you're safely back. We hadn't heard from you since you called to say Gabriella had been abducted from the garden centre. She and I were worried that something might have happened to you too.'

A likely story indeed! They didn't look in the least concerned when I came in and caught them drinking my wine. Furthermore, they could have phoned me just as easily as I could have phoned them, but did they bother? No, they didn't! As you can see, I was a bit miffed, but I wasn't going to let Richard know that. It was none of his business.

I tried to smile back at him, because after all he wasn't the villain of the piece. I didn't do very well.

'I'm all right, Richard. Nothing happened to me, but all the way home I've been imagining dreadful things that might have happened to Gabriella and it was quite a shock coming in and seeing her safe at home.' I added hastily, 'I'm so relieved she's safe. Anyway, the tea won't be long. Would you like some biscuits with it?'

'You don't seem very happy,' he said gently. 'Are you still feeling shaken up?'

Shaken up? Yes, I suppose I could truthfully tell him I was shaken up. I knew that I had been furious rather than shaken up when I first saw them together but he didn't need to know that. By this time, I had calmed down sufficiently to feel ashamed of my ill temper. Bless Richard for suggesting a more socially acceptable excuse for my snit.

'Shaken up? Yes, I suppose I must have been. I'm fine now though. Anyway, the kettle's coming to the boil. Let me just brew the tea and I'll bring it through for us all.'

In a much better frame of mind I loaded a tray with mugs, milk, sugar and teaspoons. I took a packet of shortbread out of the cupboard and added that to the tray. The kettle boiled, I made the tea and added the teapot to the tray.

'Here, you take the teapot and I'll carry the tray with the rest,' Richard said, leading the way.

'Gabs,' I said, as I followed him into the living room carrying my bright red teapot, a present she had once given me, 'I'm sorry I was a bit flummoxed when I first came in. It was quite a shock to see you there. I last saw you staggering to the car at the garden centre with a tray of geraniums. In fact I was on my way to help you load them. Then, when I got to the car, the plants were on the ground and you and the woman you were talking to had vanished. Tell me what happened. I've been imagining all kinds of dreadful things happening to you and then when I found you safe here looking as though nothing had happened, well, it shook me up a bit. What happened?'

'Well,' Gabriella was eager to tell her story, 'before I start, just for the record, I want to make one thing clear to both you and Richard.' She smiled somewhat smugly at both of us. 'I never stagger. I do not stagger even when carrying a tray of geraniums.'

How many glasses of my wine had she had?

25

Gabriella then related her experience in the back of Peggy Browne's car, emphasising her fortitude in maintaining a most uncomfortable position for the best part of an hour. She told us how she woke to find herself sprawled awkwardly across the back seat of a strange car. Her head hurt. She remembered carrying a tray of geraniums out to the car park at the garden centre but didn't remember putting them into the car. She became aware of a woman's voice coming from the driving seat. It was the woman she talked to in the garden centre. She lay still, kept her eyes closed and listened.

There was obviously an argument going on. She could only hear one end of the conversation, but from the woman's responses it was not difficult to guess what was being said on the other side of the line.

...

'You'd better be there Dave. I can't manage by myself.'

...

'Those ferries run every twenty minutes. Of course you can get there if you set off now. There's nothing to stop you.'

...

'What did you say? I don't believe it! Stop the car and bang her on the head again while she's still unconscious? Did you say that? No, Dave, I'm not doing that!'

...

'I only agreed to get her to the house, and you'd better be there.'

...

'No! Stop making excuses. I've already told you I can't bloody manage by myself.'

...

'Dave, if you're not coming, it's all off.'

...

'I'll tell you what I mean, Dave. I mean I'm not going down for you, not like those other two morons. Do you think I'm stupid? Do you?'

...

'No, Dave!'

...

'What am I going to do about it? I'll tell you what I'm going to do about it! If you're not waiting at the house when I get there, I'm going to do the same for this woman as she did for me.'

...

'She drove me to the hospital.'

...

'Try me!'

...

'This is your last chance, Dave. You'd better

be there.'

After that, Gabriella told us, the driver, who she realised straight away must be Peggy Browne, turned the radio volume back up and selected a country music station. After a few minutes she switched to light jazz. She tried a third station but didn't even get beyond a few lines of song before switching off and driving on in silence.

'You know the significance of that of course, Aggie,' This was Gabriella the psychiatrist (ret.) showing off for Richard's benefit.

'Of course,' I lied, also for Richard's benefit. 'Go on, Gabs.'

'Well, Dave Smith called again. I guessed we must be close to home or A&E by that time.'

...

'So where are you now, Dave?'

....

'You'd better be!'

...

' No! I'm not going to risk waking her up now. Do you think I'm stupid?'

...

'Don't give me that! They'll be in her bag. Where else would she put her keys?'

...

'No! I want to see your car there.'

...

'I trust you Dave, but I still want to see you. If you're not there when I get to her house I'm not going to wait for you. I'll turn the car round and go straight to A&E.'

...

'Yes, you would lie to me and I've had enough of it.'

...

Gabriella paused in her narrative for dramatic effect.

'You've no idea,' she continued, ' how uncomfortable it was in the back of that car, but I knew I had to remain apparently unconscious. It was worth it though, because I learned from the phone conversations that Peggy, who believed I was you, was bringing me back here, where she and Dave Smith would somehow persuade me to give them George's package and letter. I had my escape all planned.'

I changed the subject hastily, before she could expand on some questionable escape plan.

'Gabs, had you no idea, when you were at the garden centre, that the woman you were talking to was Peggy Browne?'.

'No, you see I'd never seen Peggy Browne close up before and I didn't pay much attention to her appearance when we were in the garden centre. She was just an elderly lady who wanted to know about plant propagation from cuttings. After I got the geraniums she said she'd walk to the car with me in case I needed any help. I thought it was nice of her.'

'Richard told me that you looked out of the window and noticed me going to the car with an old woman. He said that by the time you got there to help get the geraniums into the boot, I'd disappeared and the plants were on the ground by the car. It seems that you alerted him, and,' she turned and smiled at him, 'he had police waiting for our arrival. They handcuffed Peggy and took her away. Then Richard and I came indoors, and after a while you came back too.'

She smiled again at Richard.

'Gabs,' I said hurriedly, to divert her attention from Richard, 'I'm more relieved than I can tell you to find you safe and unhurt at home.'

She put a hand up to the back of her head and looked at me indignantly.

'Not,' I added hastily, 'that you didn't have a terribly unpleasant and frightening experience. It's just that it could have been a lot worse. For example, what if Dave Smith had been here to meet you?'

Her head couldn't have hurt too badly because the mention of Dave Smith diverted her attention immediately.

'Yes, he really let Peggy down, the rat!'

'Actually,' said Richard, 'he didn't.'

'Didn't what?'

'He didn't let Peggy down. He came here.'

We both stared at him and spoke at once.

'What do you mean? He came here? Why didn't you tell us before? Where is he now? Have the police got him too?'

'Yes, he did come here. I was watching and

saw him arrive. Either he lost his nerve or something made him suspicious. He slowed down as if to turn into your driveway, Angelina, but then accelerated away. We were hoping to catch the two of them together, but you know what they say about the best laid plans.'

I sighed. 'At least we got Peggy.'

Gabriella sighed too. 'But we didn't get the geraniums.'

26

'I've been thinking, Aggie,' my sister announced that evening over pea soup and toasted cheese sandwiches washed down, for lack of an alternative, with a merlot wine. I will not belabour the fate of the crisp white wine originally scheduled for that meal!

'Mm.' I was non-committal. You never know what my sister may be thinking.

'All this silly chasing around to recover a package and a letter that we both know doesn't exist any longer. Well, I've had an idea about how we can put a stop to it.'

She beamed expectantly, waiting for me to ask for details. Knowing Gabriella as I do though, I temporised. She always did get carried away and I was not about to rush into the first hare-brained scheme she might come up with.

'I thought your head was still hurting,' I said.

'That's just about gone. You checked my cranial nerves over yourself and said you didn't think there was any serious damage.'

'I also said I would monitor you carefully

to make sure there are no further developments,' I said firmly. 'What if you have a slow cranial haemorrhage? I think we should just have a quiet evening now and maybe talk about it tomorrow.'

'Oh, come on, don't be so daft! Slow cranial haemorrhage indeed! Don't be so stodgy. You know very well that I'm fine.'

Our discussion was interrupted by a ring from the doorbell and a rattle from the letter box. Saved by the bell I hurried to the door. On the floor below it was a white folded paper, no envelope. Expecting it to be a hand-delivered circular advertising a local service such as grass cutting, window or house cleaning I picked it up and glanced at it just in case it was offering something I needed, before throwing it into the recycling bin. But this wasn't a local circular. On it was written in untidy block capitals:

THROW THEM OUT OF THE WINDOW AT THE SIDE OF THE HOUSE.

Back in the living room my sister had taken over a crossword I'd been working on.

'Hey, Aggie,' she crowed. 'Twelve down is 'centipede' and one across was 'unfamiliar'. I'm surprised you didn't get those right away.'

She always did like to feel superior.

'Never mind that.' I handed her the paper with the message. 'Take a look at this and tell me what you think.'

She took the paper studied it.

'Throw them out of the window at the side

of the house? It doesn't say what to throw out! It doesn't say which side of the house to throw them out of either! Whoever put this through the letter box is either not very bright or too desperate to think straight. They're probably lurking out there right now.'

The same thoughts had crossed my mind. We sat in silence for a minute, then Gabriella had another thought.

'Aggie, the doors are all locked, aren't they?'

'They certainly are. Since your to-do with Ron and Mick I've been doubly careful, windows as well as doors. In fact I went round and checked them all just after dinner.'

'Right then.' Reassured of our safety Gabriella reverted to action mode. 'We need to set a trap for him. Now, what should we do? Let me think. I know, you can make up two dummy packages and two dummy letters. We'll throw one of each out of the window on both sides of the house. You can watch one side and I'll watch the other. Then we should be able to see who comes to pick them up.'

I saw flaws in this immediately. Gabriella really does get carried away. 'Then what? No Gabs, think about it. What if they're wearing balaclavas or those hoodies they always wear on television. We wouldn't recognise them. And they'd soon figure the dummy package and letter for fakes and become even more convinced that I'm hiding something important. Who knows what they'd do then? No, I'll tell you what we're going to do. We're going to call Richard.'

Gabriella, who had been none too pleased to have her brilliant plan crushed by my unassailable logic, perked up again at the prospect of involving my neighbour. She never does give up.

'Great idea! He's just the person to call.'

I called.

'Richard, you'll never guess what's just happened.'

'Actually I already know. Dave Smith triggered the alarm as he went down your driveway. I've been watching to see what he was up to and saw him stuff something through your letterbox. What was it, by the way?'

'It was a sheet of paper with a message, telling me to throw 'them', presumably the package and letter, out of a side window. Gabriella suggested I should respond with a dummy package then watch to see who picks it up. But we don't need to if you already know it's him.'

'Yes.'

'Was he on his own?'

'I didn't see anyone else go down your drive, but he might have someone waiting in a car on the street ready for a quick getaway. Unfortunately I can't see what's happening on the street from here. Anyway, he hasn't come back up the drive so I'm guessing he's still lurking around your house. You are all locked up, aren't you?'

'Oh yes, doors and windows. What do you

think we ought to do now?'

'I've already called the police so they'll be here pretty soon. I'm going to continue watching here and I'll let you know if I see him leave. Could you and your sister watch the shore road? If he sees the police arrive he might slip out over the gardens down to the shore just as he did that other time. Let's just sit tight for now and see what he does.'

Gabriella volunteered to be lookout at the living room window, and I took the bedroom at the side of the house.

'I'm not sure what we expect to accomplish, just watching out of the window,' Gabriella complained. 'I think my plan is much better, but if this is what you and Richard want, this is what we'll do.'

My mobile phone rang.

'Angelina? He's just emerged from the side of your house and he's got his phone to his ear. Oh, wait a minute, he's waving to someone by your gate, yes, he's beckoning them to join him.'

Another person joining him? This was getting worrisome. I hoped it would not be Ron or Mick. They were real thugs.

'Can you see who it is?'

'You're not going to believe this. It's a woman wearing a sleeveless dress, high heeled sandals and a ski mask! Dave is waving his arms about.'

'It's been a warm day, Richard. I'm wearing a

sleeveless top too.'

'And a ski mask?'

'No, mine's in mothballs ready for next winter. Seriously though, do you think they'll try to break into the house?'

'I doubt it but if they do I'll be right there, and the police shouldn't be long.'

The doorbell rang.

'Richard!' I hissed into the phone, 'They're at the front door. They've just rung the bell.'

'Right, go to the door,' Richard instructed calmly. 'Don't open it. Talk to them through the door. Keep them talking as long as you can. Tell them you have to know who they are and what they want before you open the door. Let them think they can persuade you to let them in.'

The doorbell rang a second time.

'Who's there?' I called through the door.

There was no reply.

'Who's there?' I called again.

A woman's voice replied, 'We're your new neighbours. We've taken over a B&B down the road.'

I recognised that voice from a week ago. It was Mrs. Walker a.k.a. Peggy Browne. The police must have released her.

'Goodness,' I replied feigning surprise, 'I hadn't heard that any of the B&Bs had been taken over. So now we have new neighbours! How long have you been here?'

'Not long, we've not been here long at all.'

'You must give me your name and your new telephone number so that I can recommend your B&B to friends.'

She replied hastily, ignoring my request for identification. 'Actually, we think you can help us. Would you mind if we come in and explain?'

I could see Gabriella coming to join me at the door looking alarmed. I put my finger to my lips, shook my head and mouthed, 'Peggy Browne.' She nodded. I turned back to the door.

'I have to be very careful about letting people in,' I called through it. 'Living alone, you see. I always like to know who's there before I open the door. You have to be careful here with all the summer visitors.'

'Oh, you don't need to worry about us. We're neighbours.'

'Actually, you do sound very nice people, but I really don't know you. You can understand why I have to be cautious. You hear of such terrible things happening.'

'You're quite right to be cautious,' Peggy replied smoothly, 'although this seems to be a very safe neighbourhood. If you don't want us to come in though, and we can understand it if you don't, then maybe you could just crack the door open a little so that we don't have to keep shouting through it.'

Gabriella, listening to the conversation, had quickly grasped what was going on. She put her finger to her lips and signalled to me that she would take over. I nodded and stepped away from the door. Our voices are very similar so I had no hesitation in letting her take over.

'Maybe I'm being ultra-cautious,' Gabriella told our visitors. 'But you see, I'm still rather shaken from something that happened to me earlier today.'

'Something that happened today? Oh dear, I hope it was nothing serious. Why don't we come in and sit down and you can tell us about it?'

'Well you see, that's the problem. I'm not sure what did happen so I can't tell you very much.'

'Do you remember anything about it?'

'It was the strangest thing. I bought some plants at a garden centre and took them to the car. The next thing I knew, I was back here leaning on the front door but without the plants.'

'That sounds very strange. Do you think it could have been just a dream?'

'No, I was definitely at the garden centre. I think I must have collapsed and someone who knew me brought me home. I do wish they had waited though, so I could see who had been so kind to me and could thank them properly. I had to get the bus back to the garden centre this afternoon to get my car. I do wish I could remember more.'

'What a nasty experience! You must be very upset. You should be sitting down instead of standing at the door. I could come in and make you a cup of tea if you like.'

'No, I'm all right thank you. But you said you need help with something. What is it that you want me to help you with?'

'It's not exactly for us. It's something for a guest staying at our B&B. Before he came to Scotland on business a couple of weeks ago he accidentally gave his secretary the wrong forwarding address. He gave her your address instead of ours. He only discovered the mistake when he phoned his office to ask about a package and a letter he had been expecting that hadn't arrived.'

I signalled Gabriella that I would take over the conversation at that point.

'You know,' I said, 'only last week someone else came here asking about a misdirected package and letter. It was the wife of the man they were sent to. Then before I could tell her about them, a window cleaner's ladder slipped and knocked her unconscious. I had to take her to A&E. I'm trying to remember her name.'

Gabriella nodded approvingly and signalled she would take over again.

'I'm very surprised,' she said, 'to hear that the package and letter that came here were important. It's a whole week since they arrived and nobody else has been to ask about them since then. I've been expecting the woman to call again for them but she hasn't done so far.'

Dave Smith took over from Peggy. He sounded impatient.

'They've been away, only got back this evening. We were going out for a walk anyway so we said we'd drop by.'

'You left guests in your B&B by themselves? Wasn't that rather risky?'

There was no reply. I took over again.

'Did you happen to see anyone else as you came along the street?' I asked innocently.

There was a brief silence before he replied.

'No.'

'Did neither of you see anyone else coming to this house just a couple of minutes before you did.'

'No. Why?'

'It's probably nothing, just some children's prank.'

'It looked like a child's writing,' Gabriella added, smothering a snicker. 'All capitals.'

'Oh,' said Peggy, quicker off the mark than Dave, 'there were some children running along the street. I didn't think you meant children. They were just playing.'

I thought it time to change the subject if we were to keep them talking.

'I'll tell you what,' I improvised, 'we really would like to meet you properly and I'm sure you'd like to meet some of the people round here too. I've had an idea. We have a regular coffee morning in the neighbourhood. Maybe one or both of you would like to come along to the next one and meet some of the people. In fact, we could even arrange to hold the next one at your B&B if that would make it easier for you. Hold on while I get a pen and paper to jot down your name and address and telephone number. I'll talk with the others and give you a call.'

There was no reply.

'What do you think?' I persisted. 'Would you be interested?'

Still no reply.

'Are you still there?'

No reply.

'Hello! Is anybody there?'

Empty silence.

Gabriella rushed to my bedroom window which overlooks the front door to see if they were still there. I heard her gasp.

'Quick, Aggie, or you'll miss it all!'

I hurried to join her and opened the window slightly.

Two policemen were striding down the driveway. Peggy was clinging onto Dave Smith as though her life depended on it. He tried to shake her off but she wouldn't let go. They were both shouting.

'Let go of me you stupid cow!' he barked at her. 'Let go, so I can get away down the garden.'

'Not on your life!' she screamed back. 'You're not running out on me again!'

'Let go, Peg. Let go or we'll both be caught.'

'No, Dave. You're not going to get away and leave me to take the rap.'

'Peg!'

'No!'

Dave and Peggy were still arguing when the police met them half way up the driveway. They were not doing anything criminal and could probably have talked their way out of the situation if they'd had their wits about them. Unfortunately for them, they hadn't. One of the policemen told them that there had been a report of prowlers in the neighbourhood and asked who they were and what they were doing.

Peggy, still wearing her ski mask, spoke up. She said they had come to my house to borrow some sugar. When asked who they had come to borrow sugar from she hesitated too long then said she thought someone lived at this house. When asked to remove her ski mask she refused, saying they didn't need to know her name or what she looked like because it was nothing to do with her and that it was all Dave's fault. When asked what was all Dave's fault she said they had better ask him because she knew nothing about it.

Dave said, 'Silly bitch!' His explanation for being there was no better. 'Don't take any notice of that silly cow. Drama queen, that's what she is. We're here because we wanted to use their telephone. Ours is out of order.'

When asked if he possessed a mobile that worked he proudly flashed one of the more expensive models in front of the two policemen, to the tune of 'Waltzing Matilda'. He said cheekily, 'Bet you two can't afford one of these.'

27

After the police car drove off with Peggy Browne and Dave Smith in the back, Gabriella and I went into the kitchen and pondered over the evening's bizarre events. After a while I told her I was going to call Richard.

'Why?' she asked, somewhat huffily I thought.

'Well, first of all to let him know that we're all right.'

'Aggie,' she sighed, 'he knows that already. If you keep calling him he'll think you're chasing after him. That puts a lot of men off, you know.'

I was aghast! The pot was surely calling the kettle black! Did she imagine I was chasing after Richard? Yes, I like him a lot, of course I do, but Gabriella was the one setting her cap at him, not me.

'Don't be silly,' I told her. 'Me chasing after Richard! Why on earth would you think such a thing?'

'Oh, just little things.'

I didn't want this conversation to continue.

'Actually,' I said hastily, 'the other reason I

have to call Richard is because there's something I want to discuss with both of you concerning the package and letter situation. I've had an idea and I want to try it out on the two of you.'

'Well try it out on me first. I told you my idea.'

'I know, but this is one that would involve all three of us, so let's see if Richard can come over.'

'Oh come on, Aggie!'

'No, I really want you both here.'

I called Richard. There was no reply. I tried again with the same result.

'Well, I can't get him on the phone right now,' I told Gabriella, 'so in the meantime I think I'm going to go out and see if there's a car parked up on the street. Dave Smith and Peggy Browne must have come in one and it should still be there. I want to take a good look at it and see if it looks anything like the one that was parked next to us at the garden centre. You know, the black one you were abducted in. Are you coming?'

'Of course I am. I know what it looks like. I remember the inside of it very well too. Let me get my shoes on.'

I don't know why we tiptoed up the drive. We knew very well that the police had taken Dave and Peggy away. Maybe it was a sixth sense. It was a good thing we did keep quiet though because as we approached the gate we could hear voices coming from the street. We stayed where we were on the drive, screened from the street by the shrubbery, and listened. We knew those voices well.

'This is the last bloody thing I'm doing for 'im.'

'Aye.'

''E told me 'e gets the money on Wednesday. 'E'd better bloody pay us then.'

'Aye.'

'Mebbe we should go back to York after that.'

'Aye, mebbe. When we get the money.'

...

''Old on a minute. Did you 'ear something just then? I 'eard a noise coming from those bushes, a rustling, like.'

'Shurrup while I 'ave a listen.'

Gabriella and I held our breath. There was indeed a rustle by our feet and a black shadow leaped through the bushes and out onto the street.

'A bloody cat. That's what you 'eard Mick, a bloody cat.'

'Aye well, let's not 'ang about any longer. Let's get away from 'ere.'

We heard car doors opening and waited to hear the engine fire up. There was silence. A car door opened again and we could hear one of the men get out, then the other.

'You stupid bugger!'

'I thought you 'ad it.'

'Don't be daft, 'Ow could I 'ave it? Dave 'ad it 'imself to drive 'ere, didn't 'e?. 'E told me to look for the spare one.'

'Oh aye. You didn't tell me that, did you? I thought 'e would 'ave left it in t'ignition. Where is it then? Where did 'e say the spare one is?'

"E said nowt about where it is, 'e just said we 'ad to use the spare one. Then 'e said 'e 'ad to go and rang off.'

'So 'e didn't tell you where 'e keeps the spare one, then.'

'No, I told you, 'e rang off before I could ask 'im.'

"Go and 'ave a look in the pocket then. If it's not there, look under the floor mat.'

'I already looked in both them places when we were in the car. I'm not daft, you know.'

'Right, let's go 'ome. Let bloody Dave get 'is own bloody car back.'

'Nay, we've got to get it back for 'im 'aven't we? 'E won't pay us if we don't do what 'e tells us. 'Ang on a minute though, I've 'ad a thought.'

'Oh aye.'

'Feel under the mudguards, run your fingers just under the edge. 'E might 'ave one of those magnet things you can put a spare key in. In case you need it, like. I'll do this side, you do that one.'

'There's a lot of muck under 'ere.'

'Aye, but keep looking.'

'I can feel a sort of box under 'ere. Do you think this might be it?'

'Pull it off and see. 'Ere give it to me. Let's 'ave a look.'

'Nay, I can open it. Aye, this'll be it. It's got a key inside right enough. Come on, let's go.'

We heard car doors opening and closing and they were away. As Gabriella said, they didn't waste any time once they found the key.

Richard emerged from behind the shrubs.

'I thought that cat was going to give us away,' he said.

'Well, hello,' I replied. 'Have you been here all the time? I tried to phone you but you didn't answer.'

'I left my phone in the house. Good thing I did, wasn't it?'

'Well yes, I suppose so. Actually Richard, the reason I was trying to call you is that I've had an idea about how we can put an end to all this. I want to sound it out on you and Gabriella. Do you have time to come in and see what you think about it?'

'I've always got time for you, Angelina,' he replied gallantly.

Gabriella looked at him sharply. I can't be sure because he turned away quickly, but I think he went a little pink.

'Come on, then.' I included both of them in a wave of my arm. 'I'll put on a pot of coffee.'

28

'Right, Aggie.' Gabriella was comfortably settled in an armchair with coffee in one hand and shortbread in the other. 'We're ready to listen.'

She indicated the plate of shortbread. 'You can leave that on the table here.'

Richard, seated in the other armchair nodded his approval of my sister's suggestion. 'Good thinking, Gabriella.'

'If you're sure you're both ready,' I said to bring them back to the topic in hand. 'I want to see what you both think about an idea I have.'

I got their half attention at least.

'I've been thinking about all this,' I began, 'and I believe it began over money. And therefore money may be the key to ending it.'

Neither Gabriella nor Richard seemed particularly impressed by my statement but listened anyway while they sipped their coffee.

I pressed on. 'Everything started with someone at the military base leaking classified information on the web. George and his team came up to the base to investigate. They sent dummy investigative reports in a package and a letter to my address. The perpetrator knew these reports had been sent and must have been desperate to intercept them. To do this though, he needed help from someone off base. He somehow, directly or indirectly, was able to contact Dave Smith and offer him a finder's fee to retrieve them.

'Shortly after that, the perpetrator was apprehended at the base and taken into custody there. We're told that he admitted he was paid to leak the information. This of course would be why he was in a position to offer money to Dave Smith. Once the perpetrator was taken into custody though, and the reports no longer mattered, he was unable to contact Dave to tell him not to bother retrieving them.

'Dave Smith hasn't been contacted so still assumes he'll be getting his finder's fee. Now as Richard told us, Dave isn't one to risk his own skin, so he in turn has offered a finder's fee to other people to retrieve the package and letter. These people are still looking for them, believing they'll be paid when they find them.' 'That's a fair overview of the situation as we know it Angelina,' Richard commented gravely.

I noticed his careful choice of words. It crossed my mind that he might know something we didn't, but wasn't about to tell us. I think Gabriella probably thought the same thing, as twins sometimes do, because she was looking at him very speculatively. When he didn't say any more she turned back to me.

'You said you've got an idea you want to try out on us, Aggie. You haven't actually told us what it is yet.'

'Yes, well my idea is simply this. The finder's fee offered to Dave must
be pretty substantial for him to be able to dangle enough money in front of Ron and Mick and Peggy to make them go to the lengths they have to find George's package and letter. Think about it. When those students with their silly window cleaning ruse failed to get them by petty theft, and Peggy, posing as Mrs John Walker, failed to get them by coming to the door and asking nicely for them, there was enough money in it for Dave to call in the heavies, Ron and Mick. Think of the risks those two took. They knocked me unconscious while they ransacked the house. When they spotted me accidentally in York they turned over my hotel room. We've seen them come back to the house and they'd probably have broken in again if the police hadn't arrived.

'Then there was the garden centre episode. Peggy Browne followed my car to the garden centre, mistook Gabs for me, banged her on the head, then brought her back here for Dave to have a go himself. Fortunately for Gabs that plan fell apart. So then, this evening Dave and Peggy risked coming to the house yet again despite the fact that the police had been called on two previous occasions.'

'So what's the great plan? You still haven't

told us.'

Gabriella always did nit-pick.

'Well, isn't it obvious?' I said. 'None of them give two pins for the package and letter. All they want is the money. Dave Smith promised payment when he himself is paid. As long as he still expects to be paid the search will go on.'

'Fine,' Gabriella continued to pick holes in my idea, 'you're suggesting we pay them off, aren't you? Do you know how much money you're talking about? Do you know who needs to be paid, and how much was promised? Do you know how to contact them? And anyway, where would money to pay them off come from?'

'Why, George of course. He started the whole thing by sending the package and letter here. He had access to funds to put my house right after Ron and Mick trashed it. I'll just bet he'll have access to funds to settle the payoffs too.'

I looked at Richard. 'Won't he?'

'I say Dave Smith doesn't deserve a penny!' Gabriella jumped in.

'I agree with you,' I said. 'But do you really want to get hit on the head and carted off in a the back of a Vauxhall again? There's no telling what they might try next.'

'And anyway,' Gabriella was still indignant on her son's behalf, 'what if Dave Smith just keeps the money himself and doesn't tell Ron and Mick that the search is off? What then?'

Richard intervened. 'Let's not get ahead of

ourselves. Angelina's idea does have merit, but the devil would of course be in the details. Leave it with me to talk it over with George and see if he thinks something could be worked.'

'Don't bother, I'll just call George myself and tell him!' Gabriella was back in action mode now there was something to be done. 'He started it all so it's only right that he should help clean up the mess.'

He's already cleaned my house up, and very well too.' I pointed out. 'He may not be in a position to do any more.'

'Please, Gabriella,' Richard said urgently, 'and you too Angelina, please don't on any account try to contact George. Please, please remember you were told of his involvement in the strictest confidence.'

'I don't see how you could have avoided telling us about his involvement,' Gabriella grumbled, 'given the circumstances.'

'Yes well, maybe. Nevertheless, you were told in confidence and you agreed to that.'

It was time for me to intervene. 'Yes we did and we'll honour it, won't we Gabs. Now, coffee refills for anyone?'

29

The telephone rang while we were having breakfast the following morning. It was Richard. Gabriella couldn't hide her delight when I signalled her to pick up the extension. We both anticipated some kind of invitation, if only to go over for coffee. Richard however wasted no time on small talk.

'Angelina, if you don't mind I need you and your sister to get away from here as quickly as you can. Take whatever clothes and things you need for the next few days, and leave straight away. Plan on staying away until I tell you it's safe to come back. I don't want you to try to contact either me or George but I do promise to call you on your mobile and let you know when it's safe for you to come back. All right?'

Gabriella and I stared at each other.

'What's happening Richard? Why do you want us out of the way?' I asked. 'We're not refusing to go, we'll do as you ask, but I want to know why. Are you expecting some kind of trouble?'

'Not exactly. Just trust me on this. I'll explain later but there's no time right now. I'd like you to leave this morning, the sooner the better. Can you do that?'

'Yes of course we can if it's that urgent. Don't worry, we'll be gone before you know it.'

'Just watch us!' Gabriella added.

We rushed to our respective bedrooms and each threw together a few days' supply of clothes and toiletries. We were out of the house and into the car and on the coast road to the ferry in just over ten minutes.

'Just like when we left York in a hurry,' Gabriella recollected as we drove along. 'I hope we packed everything we need, but we can always buy anything we forgot. I do wonder what Richard's expecting to happen though.'

I joined the queue of cars waiting at the ferry terminal. We could discuss where to go during the twenty-minute ferry crossing. I didn't mind where we went so was happy to let my sister choose.

'Your turn to decide where to go, Gabs.'

'Well, if you remember, you were on your way to come and stay with me at Bungay a week ago, so why don't we just go there now? I left home in such a hurry to join you in York I had to leave things just as they were. There's probably sour milk in the fridge by now. We can pick up groceries and anything else we need at one of the supermarkets on the way. We've set off early enough so we can either do the whole journey today or, if you would prefer it, we could stop somewhere overnight and break the journey. Fancy another night in York?'

I most certainly did not feel like stopping overnight in York again.

'Let's just drive on,' I said. 'It'll be easy enough with the two of us sharing the driving. We have to stop to eat anyway so that'll break the journey up.'

We did stop at a couple of motorway restaurants en route. The fare was not exciting but perfectly adequate, sausage and chips at one stop and fruit pie at the other. We detoured via Cambridge to collect Gabriella's car, a shiny new red Audi which she had left there with a friend when she took the train to come and meet me in York. She suggested we stock up with food in Cambridge. This accomplished, she set off on the road for Bungay in her Audi with a quite unnecessary vroom and I followed in my trusty Beetle.

Gabriella didn't waste any time when we arrived at her house. She went straight out into her garden to water her thirsty plants. First things first! Meanwhile I set about preparing a salad with cold cuts we had picked up in Cambridge. I was glad we had decided to come to her peaceful house, despite the long drive. Nothing unexpected was likely to happen there, which was more than could be said right then of my house back in Dunoon.

It was a lovely evening, so after we cleared away the remnants of dinner I suggested a good long walk to stretch our legs after sitting in the car all day.

'Good idea!' Gabriella was enthusiastic. 'We can finish up at the pub round the corner from the house. I don't like to go on my own, but I often take guests there. The two of us together will be fine. I think you'll enjoy it.'

She knew all her local walks and we strolled for a good hour before ending up at the pub. I found I was quite thirsty and looked forward to sitting down with a long drink.

'This is my treat,' Gabriella declared when we went in. 'What would you like?'

'I'd like a vodka and tonic with a twist of lime,' I told her. 'But in a tall glass filled right up with tonic please. I'm pretty thirsty.'

Gabriella glanced round the room. Her quick eye noticed some people picking their things up off one of the tables, obviously preparing to leave.

'Quick Aggie, you go and grab that little table over by the window,' she said. 'The folks are just leaving. I'll bring the drinks across. We're lucky to get a table tonight. Hurry, the pub's really busy.'

I went straight to the table being vacated and laid claim to it.

I wasn't deliberately listening in on a nearby conversation, but the little tables were huddled together and the middle-aged couple sitting at the one next to me were not exactly whispering. I pricked up my ears when I became aware they were talking about mutual acquaintances. When Gabriella came over with the drinks I put a warning finger to my lips and nodded slightly in the direction of the couple to indicate that she should listen too.

'... really thinking of going back to York for good then, are they?'

'Yes well, you know our Ron. Likes to be near the family he does. Mick'll go wherever he goes. Always did. Follows our Ron round like a puppy, does Mick.'

Gabriella looked at me, horrified. She mouthed, 'Ron and Mick? York?'

I nodded slowly then waved my glass at her and said, 'Cheers!'

'Cheers!' she responded, clinking her glass against mine.

There was a lot of background noise from conversations round the room but the couple were close enough for us to hear much of what they were saying. We sipped our drinks slowly to make them last, anxious not to appear to be listening but in fact straining to hear every word. Not all their conversation revolved round Ron and Mick of course. What we did we hear, though, was enough:

'Mick's the youngest, isn't he?'

'Aye, he's the baby of the family and the daftest. Nearly set the house on fire at Mam's birthday party. I'd already put one of those single candles that says 60 on the cake.'

'I thought you told me she was sixty-three.'

'She was, but sixty was the nearest I could find. Anyway, that wasn't good enough for our Mick. He went and bought four packets of twenty of those little candles they put on kids' birthday cakes and took my big 60 candle off and put sixty-three of his little ones on instead. Then he tried to light them and the whole thing went up in flames.'

'Did it do much damage?'

'Only to the cake and Mam's best table-cloth. We had to empty the teapot over it to put out the fire. It was a good thing we were using the big teapot for all the family. The little one Mam usually uses would have been useless. But that's Mick for you. Means well, but doesn't think.'

'... Are they still in Scotland, then, or have they already gone back to York?'

'They were still in Scotland when Ron phoned Mam last night. She phoned me and told me this morning. He told Mam that they're just waiting to be paid for a job they've been working on, then they're going back to York.'

'What kind of job were they doing up there?'

'Ron told Mam it was top-secret military work. He said it was work of national importance and he wasn't allowed to tell anyone, so Mam hasn't to tell anyone what he told her. Mam says I mustn't tell Ron that she told me and I haven't to tell anyone else, so you'd better not tell anyone either.'

'I wouldn't have thought they'd trust those two with top-secret work. I wonder what it's about. Didn't Ron tell your Mam any more than that?'

'He couldn't, could he? It's secret.'

'I still find it hard to believe that those two are secret agents. They just don't seem to be the type, if you know what I mean.'

'I know what you mean but you're wrong. Our Ron's got brains, you know. He's not daft.'

'Mebbe not, but he's a bit handy with his fists. Short fuse has Ron. Don't get me wrong, I'm not saying anything against him, but I would have thought you'd have to have a cool head for top secret work. Mebbe a university degree as well, you know, just to be considered for the job.'

There was a pause, presumably while the woman thought about that.

'Well, they must have needed a special kind of secret agent for something or other and our Ron and Mick just happened to fit the bill. I bet they have all different kinds of people working on national security. Oh and by the way, Ron asked about us and said to wish us a good holiday and we might be hearing from him. He's thoughtful like that is our Ron.'

'Aye, mebbe. I wonder what they've been doing up in Scotland though. It must be something important.'

'We can ask them when we see them at York

races. They never miss the races. We can ask our Mam as well once they're back in York. Mick tells her everything.'

'Aye. Last time we went to the races your Mick had some good tips. Mebbe he'll have some more this time.'

The couple did not discuss brothers Ron and Mick further, but we heard enough in the pub to be certain which Ron and Mick were being talked about. As we left, Gabriella and I agreed we should call Richard, despite his instructions, to tell him about the brothers' intention to leave Scotland as soon as they were paid.

When we called Richard, however, all we got was an invitation to leave a message on his voice-mail. We did so, expecting he would call back that evening, but he didn't.

30

I was anxious to know what was happening in Dunoon and why it was necessary for us to leave. This was the second time Richard had practically chased me out of my house without explanation. I told Gabriella I had half a mind to go back without waiting for him to call. She told me not to be silly, pointing out that even when he did call there was nothing to hurry back for. She was right of course, in her case at any rate but just possibly not in mine.

'Let's just take off and enjoy the day,' she said. 'Let's go and explore the John Constable countryside. You always enjoy that. We'll use my car. It's more stylish and much more comfortable than your old Beetle.'

Gabriella always did like to score points.

We drove to Flatford Mill, parked the car and wandered round. I was familiar with the scenery from previous visits as well as from Constable's paintings. I decided to take some snapshots. My camera was still in Dunoon so I delved in my purse for my mobile, which takes better photos than my camera anyway. It wasn't there, it was still plugged in on its charger in Gabriella's spare bedroom.

'Can I borrow your mobile to take a few pictures?' I asked.

'I didn't bring it,' she replied airily. 'I never take it out with me. I don't want it ringing in the supermarket and I don't like having to hear other peoples' conversations on their phones.'

I didn't argue. She was just showing off. She knows very well how to turn her mobile on and off. I should have remembered to bring my own.

It was early for lunch but the car park of a nearby restaurant was already beginning to fill up. We guessed that implied a reputation for quality fare, so went in.

'You go ahead,' Gabriella said. 'I just need to spend a penny. I'll catch you up.'

One of the advantages of going to a restaurant early is having a choice of table. I opted for one by the window and watched more diners drive into the car park. A grey car pulled into one of the slots. The couple getting out were the people whose conversation we overheard in the pub in Bungay the previous evening. It shouldn't have worried me but it did. I wanted to warn Gabriella to not show any sign of recognising them as she came in. They had no reason to remember us, because we had avoided drawing attention to ourselves in the pub, but people often notice identical twins. However, neither of us had our mobiles with us so I just held the wine list in front of my face as the couple were escorted past me to another table.

'Could we have that table by the window?' I heard the woman ask.

They were led in my direction. I kept my face hidden while chairs shuffled behind me.

Gabriella appeared in the doorway and spotted me. Before I could stop her she waved and called, 'Oh great, Aggie! You got us a table by the window. I was hoping you would. I've been talking to people out there and they said everything on the menu here is really good. You can't go wrong, whatever you order.'

'That's good news,' a female voice came from the table behind me, 'I can't wait to see the menu.'

Without thinking, I turned.

The woman looked quizzically at me. 'Why, I know I've seen you somewhere before. I'm just trying to remember where.'

Then, as Gabriella turned too, 'Oh my, are you twins? Look Jim, aren't these two ladies alike?'

The man looked carefully at us.

'I know where we saw you,' he said. 'You were in the pub last night. I remember noticing when you got up to leave. I noticed then how much alike you are. I didn't think about it at the time but now Sheila points it out, yes, I can see that you're twins. Well, now we've met, I'm Jim and this is Sheila. Do you live round here?'

Gabriella was quick off the mark. 'Yes,' she said. 'Bungay, where you saw us last night. I'm Gabby and this is Aggie.'

I noticed she avoided giving our full names. Before Jim could ask any more she redirected the conversation. 'What about yourselves, are you from these parts too, or are you visiting?'

'Half and half. We live in York. Do you know it? Lovely city. Sheila's from there, still has family there. I'm from Yarmouth originally so we like to come here sometimes. We stay at B&Bs.'

Keeping the conversation away from ourselves, I said, 'It seems most people are going abroad for their holidays nowadays.'

'We've been to ... '

The waiter appeared at the table to take to take our orders. Gabriella and I excused ourselves and turned back to our own table. We didn't attempt to continue our conversation with Sheila and Jim after that, and neither did they. Remembering their conversation in the pub the previous evening though, we kept our ears pricked for further mention of Sheila's brothers. It was a good thing we did. We had already finished our seafood salads and were waiting for the bill. In fact, I had given up hope of overhearing any more about them when Jim broached the subject.

'Sheila, didn't I hear you on the phone to your Mam this morning?'

'Yes, I called her while you were putting our coats and things in the car. You know she likes me to call her every day when we're away. Says it puts her mind at rest. I didn't call any earlier though because she always says if there's bad news she wants it after breakfast, not before. Not that I had any bad news of course, but that's Mam for you.'

'Had she heard any more from Ron and Mick?'

'Yes, Ron was asking after us. Wasn't that nice of him to think of us. Ooh yes, I nearly forgot, there was a message ... '

Sheila's passing on the message was interrupted by the arrival of the waiter with the dessert trolley. Naturally this took precedence over the message. Choices made, the trolley was wheeled to our table.

'Maybe later,' we told the waiter. The trolley moved and our neighbours settled down to their desserts. We listened shamelessly.

'This is so good, I'm wondering whether to have another.'

'You'll be putting on weight if you do.'

'What about you? Are you going to have any more?'

'No, and I don't think you should either.'

'All right. They were good though, weren't they.'

'Yes they were. But just before the sweets came you said your Mam had a message for us from Ron.'

'Oh yes, I was forgetting. Ron wants us to look out for a woman driving an old blue Beetle.

He heard she was going to Bungay. If we see her we have to call him.'

'I knew it. As soon as you said he'd been asking about us I knew Ron must want us to do something for him. He'll have to pay us though. What else did your Mam say?'

'Nothing. She wouldn't, would she, not if it's top secret.'

'Didn't you ask her?'

'Well, I know she'd have told me if she knew. All she said was that we should tell Ron if we see the car and the woman.'

'If Ron wants us to spend our holiday spying for him, he'll have to pay us. We'd better find out how much. See if it's worth it.'

'It won't hurt to keep our eyes open though. Then if Ron won't pay us anything we needn't tell him. What if this woman's a secret agent on the other side? What if she's stolen some important documents, you know, matters of national importance? Fancy bringing them all the way from Scotland to Bungay. We'd better keep a look out. You look at cars, Jim. Have you seen any old blue Beetles round here?

'No, I can't say I've noticed any. In fact, there don't seem to be that many older cars about nowadays. But you're right, we'll watch out from now on, starting with the car park outside. Then maybe we could go to Bungay and see if we spot one there.'

31

I was aghast. Sheila and Jim were going to look for an older blue Beetle. Thank goodness we were using Gabriella's Audi. We wouldn't be rumbled immediately if they started searching in the car park outside. However, my blue Beetle was parked in her driveway in full view of the road. Not only that, but she had told Sheila and Jim we were from Bungay. We had to get back home and get the Beetle into Gabriella's garage before they headed there.

The restaurant car park was laid out in neat rows so we knew it wouldn't take the pair of them more than a few minutes to check there. It was imperative that we leave the restaurant right away. I signalled the waiter to bring our bill. No desserts for us that day! To my horror, as he approached our table I heard Jim's voice behind me,

'You can bring ours at the same time, if you wouldn't mind.'

I turned to see Jim waving to him.

'I'll be right back, sir.' Turning to me, the waiter said, 'Sorry to keep you waiting, ma'am.' He waved a notepad in his hand, signalling he was about to take an order at another table.

Gabriella, who I have to say can be very quick on the uptake, stood and picked up her jacket from the back of her chair. 'We'll just pay at the desk,' she called to the waiter.

We both rose and collected our jackets and bags. He turned and looked at her gratefully. 'Thank you, ma'am, we're in a bit of a rush at the moment.' He turned to Jim. 'I won't be long with yours, sir.'

We said goodbye to Jim and Sheila as we left our table and wished them good weather for the rest of their holiday. By tacit agreement we were careful not to give the appearance of being in a hurry as we walked to the reception desk to pay our bill. Thankfully, they stayed and waited for their bill to be brought to them. We drove straight home.

'Do you have your car keys with you?' Gabriella asked as we neared the house. 'I've had an automatic opener fitted on the garage door since you were last here so if you've got your keys you can jump out and drive your car straight in.'

'Yes, I've got them here. They live in my handbag.'

I fished the keys out of my bag so as to be ready to move the Beetle. I had been telling Gabriella she should have an automatic opener fixed on her garage door for the last few years. Thank goodness she had done it at last.

We turned into her driveway and pulled up

behind the Beetle. She clicked open the garage door with a flourish. I leapt out of the Audi, unlocked my car and drove it quickly into the garage.

With my dear little Beetle safely out of sight from the road, Gabriella asked, 'Where would you like to go this afternoon? We could go to the coast but since you live on the west coast of Scotland, that might not be much of a treat. You know the area. Where shall we go?'

'How about Norwich?' I suggested. 'Cambridge would be nice too but I seem to remember the traffic can be awful getting there. We once got stuck behind a tractor or something for miles. I'd say, let's do Norwich today. I think we should stay well away from Bungay the rest of the day and avoid Jim and Sheila if they come snooping round here looking for the Beetle.'

We spent a few hours walking round Norwich. We went into the cathedral as we always do, looked once again at the *danse macabre* painting with its morbid warning and listened to some organ music. We also spent time in the shops, which I enjoyed because they were a change from my own ones at home. I told Gabriella I would treat us both to dinner if she would select the restaurant. She said thanks but no thanks because she had a few things she needed to do at home.

'You can treat us another day,' she said. 'How about soup and sandwiches at mine?'

'Fine with me, we've already had a good lunch today so that sounds fine.'

There was a grey car parked on the road outside Gabriella's house when we got back.

'Turn into your driveway as you normally do,' I whispered to Gabriella. I don't know why I was whispering but I did. Furthermore, she whispered back.

'Right. Good thinking. They've had all day to discover I live here and my Audi will imply that we're not the type of people to be driving a disreputable old Beetle.'

She never misses a chance to disparage my car, but it has been well looked after and is good for at least another hundred thousand miles, maybe twice that.

The grey car moved off as we turned into Gabriella's driveway. She said it was not one that belonged to any of her neighbours. We couldn't see who was inside so it could have been Sheila and Jim or it could just as easily have been someone else. We parked the Audi on the drive and went into the house. We kept an eye on the road outside but did not see the grey car again that evening.

32

'I'm going to walk down to the post office later on, Aggie,' Gabriella told me as we cleared away after breakfast the following day. 'I'll pick up something nice for lunch as well. I shouldn't be much more than an hour or so. Do you want to come with me or would you prefer to stay home?'

'I think I'll stay here if you don't mind. I picked out one of your books to read last night and I want to finish it while I'm still here.'

'You don't have to finish it while you're here you know, you can take it back home with you when you go. There's no hurry, you can give it back when you next see me.'

'I know, but part of being on holiday is sitting down with a good book at times when you'd normally be doing other things. You go and do your errands and I'll stay here and have a good read.'

'OK. Do you want me to get you anything while I'm out?'

'No, I'm fine thanks. You might keep an eye out for Jim and Sheila though. They're bound to be prowling round Bungay sometime, in fact today more than likely. Remember the grey car that was parked along the road when we got home yesterday? It might not have been them, of course, but then again it might. I was also thinking that maybe we should cover my Beetle up with a blanket or something, so that if they come here snooping they won't be able to see it through the garage window.'

'I suppose we could,' Gabriella mused. 'But then it would look as though we have something hidden under the cover, something the size and shape of a car. I mean, why would anyone cover up an old jalopy inside a garage and leave a beautiful new car outside uncovered?'

I didn't want to start the day with an argument so refrained from pointing out that if a car is covered up there is no way to tell its age and condition so there could be no comparison between the one covered and the one uncovered.

'That's true, Gabs,' I conceded. 'But I've just had another idea. You know Jim's tall enough to peer in through the window. Well, what if we block it, you know, hang a cloth or something over it?'

Gabriella looked doubtful.

Twins often know what the other is thinking. 'No,' I said. 'Now I come to think about it, that might not be such a good idea either. Covering the window up might look suspicious. The whole point of a window is to be able to see through it.'

'Hold on a minute, you're absolutely right.

We do need to block the window. And I know just how to do it. Listen, there's a bookshelf along the wall that I keep empty pots and things on. We can push it under the window and stand some plants on it. I've got some cuttings in pots outside that are getting nice and leafy. I put them out on a shelf at the back of the house to acclimatise a couple of weeks ago. Come and help me move the bookcase, then we'll carry some to the garage and cram them inside the window. Come on.'

The scheme worked beautifully. The leafy cuttings not only filled the window, they blocked the daylight so it made the garage too dark to be able to see anything inside. Fantastic! My brilliant sister! Gabriella always was resourceful as well as having green thumbs. My trusty Beetle was now well protected from prying eyes.

I decided to go with her after all. It was too nice a day to stay indoors reading. We were on the way home from our shopping when a grey car, which looked suspiciously like the one we has noticed the previous evening, drove past. It slowed down and waited for us to catch up. Sheila, in the passenger seat, lowered her window and called:

'Hello there! Nice to see you again. Do you remember talking to me and Jim yesterday in that restaurant where we had lunch? We did introduce ourselves but I'm sorry, I'm not much good at remembering names. She looked at me. 'Are you Greta, or maybe Agnes? Never mind, I expect you're used to people mixing you up.'

We had overheard enough the previous day to know that Jim and Sheila were not in Bungay by accident.

'Anyway,' Sheila continued, 'Jim and I saw you walking along the road just now and remembered you. Actually though, we're wondering if you can help us since you live here.'

'I'll help if I can,' Gabriella, the resident, said. 'By the way, did you have a nice time yesterday? You were still in the restaurant when we left. Did you go somewhere nice after that? You had lovely weather.'

'Oh we just toured around, but have you … '

Gabriella cut her off before she could finish.

'Yes, I like touring round too. Is that what you're doing again today? I'm afraid it won't take you long to look round Bungay, but there are lots of other nice places to see. I daresay you know of them. Well, Jim will because he's from these parts. Anyway, I'm sure you'll have a lovely time. Well, I have to get on. It was nice seeing you again. Enjoy the day.'

Then, as if it were an afterthought she added, 'Oh, I'm forgetting, you were asking for help with something. Do you need directions? I can probably help you there.'

Sheila was getting impatient with all this trivia. Good, she would be more likely to let something slip.

'No, we know our way around pretty well, thank you. We don't need directions. Actually, we're looking for a particular car, an older model blue Beetle. Do you, by any chance, have one?'

Was that a shot in the dark?

'No I don't.'

'Have you noticed one driving around Bungay recently?

'I'm perfectly sure none of my neighbours have a blue Beetle. Why on earth are you looking for one?'

Sheila didn't have an answer. I noticed her nudge Jim, who promptly came to her rescue.

'Oh, I'm a long time Beetle enthusiast,' he said. 'I saw a woman driving an older blue one near Bungay one day while we were touring round. I'd like to take a picture of it for my collection.'

'Goodness, why ever didn't you take a picture of it right away when you saw it?' Gabriella asked innocently.

'Sadly, I didn't have my camera with me.'

'I take pictures with my mobile phone.' Gabriella continued to play her part. 'Maybe you should get one like mine, then you don't have to worry about carrying a camera.'

There was no reply to this so after a pause she continued, 'Well I'm afraid I don't own a blue Beetle and I can't say that I've seen any of my neighbours driving one either. I wonder where you saw it?'

She leaned close to the car and addressed Jim, 'Do you collect the numbers to go with the photographs? I suppose you have to photograph them at the right angle to take in the number plate.'

Jim ignored her question. He looked away, shrugged and restarted his engine.

'Thanks anyway,' he said. 'We just thought we'd ask.'

'Bye,' added Sheila.

The car moved off and we continued on our way home.

'You should have gone into acting instead of medicine' I told Gabriella when they'd gone.

'Yes, I thought I did rather well,' she replied airily. She always was a show-off.

'I bet they don't give up though,' I said. 'I bet they start asking other people and sooner or later they'll discover that you live alone in Bungay and the twin sister is visiting from Scotland. I do wish Richard would call so we can tell him what's going on here.'

He didn't telephone that morning, but my nephew George did.

'I've got a few days between assignments, Mum, so how would it be if I come and spend them with you?'

Gabriella was overjoyed of course. George would sort things out.

'Oh George, you just don't know how glad I'll be to see you! I'm so relieved you're coming. When can I expect you?'

'Maybe three hours. Less, depending on the traffic. I'll be coming in a rental car so you can save your petrol while I'm there. Your car can stay in the garage.'

'Right, er, we'll have to talk about that when you get here. Shall I save you some lunch?'

'That'll be great Mum. If you save me something I won't stop to eat on the way. See you!'

He rang off before Gabriella had a chance to tell him any more.

'Typical George!' she exclaimed. 'Fancy ringing off like that!'

I refrained from pointing out the old truism, 'The apple doesn't fall far from the tree'.

We decided it would be best to stay home until he arrived, rather than go out. It would be silly to risk bumping into Jim and Sheila again if they were still in Bungay. The last thing we wanted was to be quizzed again about my Beetle. I settled down to my book with my mobile close by, in case Richard should ring. Gabriella went out to potter in her back garden.

I was deep in my book and she was still out in her garden when I heard raised voices coming through the slightly open window from the driveway outside. Looking out I saw George and Jim.

'... and we have to assess the damage before we can give the lady a price.'

'I don't see any damage on the garage. What precisely did the lady ask you to look at?'

'We're doing an inspection for dry rot.'

'This is a brick garage.'

'There might be some round the window

frame.'

'I can assure you there is not.'

'It'll be on the inside. Look at all those plants keeping the wood damp. That'll do it.'

'I don't know what you're up to but I think you'd better leave.'

'Who are you to tell me what to do?'

Then I heard Gabriella exclaim, 'That's George's voice!' as she rushed from the back to greet him. I went out to join them.

'George! How lovely to see you again.'

'Hello Mum! Hi Aunt Aggie!'

I looked at Jim, who was quietly walking away, and called, 'Jim! Did you come for something?'

He did not reply.

'Jim!' Gabriella called.

He did not look back.

'Don't worry, Mum,' George said. 'Let him go. I've taken pictures of him and his car and of the woman in it as well so we'll be keeping an eye on them.'

I was curious. 'Why did you take pictures of them? I'm glad you did, but I do wonder what inspired you to take them. Do you know something?'

George laughed. 'No. I'm just routinely cautious. As I arrived, the car ahead of me pulled up outside your house and I saw the man you called Jim get out and go straight to the your garage. I was suspicious because of all you hear about rogue traders. Then when I saw him try the handle of the garage and it wouldn't open I knew something must be going on because Mum never used to have a lock on the garage. What on earth is she hiding in there? I know it's not her car because that's parked out here on the drive. I tried to look in through the window but it's blocked with a load of plants.'

'Come inside, George, we've a lot to tell you.'

33

When George called his mother, suggesting he come and spend a few days with her, he had not been sure whether she would be back in Bungay or still staying with me up in Scotland. When she verified she was back home, he simply told her he was setting off right away and would arrive in a couple of hours or so. He rang off before Gabriella had time to tell him that I was occupying the second of her two bedrooms and he would be sleeping on the sofa. I heard her explain this to him as they came into the house. Despite the prospect of sleeping on the sofa, he greeted me warmly.

'Hey, Aunt Aggie, I wasn't expecting to see you so soon. Are you sick of your beautifully refurbished house already?'

I explained how, on Richard's advice, we had left my beautifully refurbished house in a hurry and been told not to return until he contacted me again to say it was safe. I said I was still anxiously waiting to be told I could go home.

'Right,' George nodded, 'I'll get to the bottom of whatever's going on up in Scotland. Now, what about what's going on here? What about that little incident just as I arrived, Mum? You do realise that man you called Jim was trying to see into your garage, don't you? What have you got hidden in there?'

Gabriella handed him a plate of sandwiches and a napkin. 'Here's your lunch, George. I hope we saved you enough. You get started on that while I make us all a pot of tea. It won't take me a minute. Then we can sit down and tell you what's been happening. We've quite a lot to tell you.'

George, it transpired, had been out of the country and was unaware of the further attempts to find the long-since destroyed package and letter since he left Dunoon. We told him how glad we were that he had left his surveillance system up on my driveway and how it had alerted Richard to the various attempts to get into my house. Between us, we told him how we had watched from next door to see Dave Smith come to the house with Ron and Mick only to find it locked and no one there to answer the doorbell. We told him how Richard had called the police and how Dave had slipped away and left Ron and Mick on their own to explain what they were doing at my house. Presumably, the pair gave an acceptable explanation because they were not detained.

We told him about Gabriella's adventure, or rather misadventure, at the garden centre, how she was knocked unconscious and abducted by Peggy Browne in the garden centre car park, dragged into a car and driven back to my house.

Gabriella the drama queen thoroughly enjoyed telling him how she had recovered consciousness in the car and listened in on Peggy's call to Dave, so was not worried because she had planned her escape. She told him how Peggy had then abandoned her outside the front door because Dave was not waiting for them at the house.

George looked increasingly worried as Gabriella happily told her tale. He pointed out that if I hadn't happened to look out of the garden centre window just as Gabriella had been dragged into the car, and had called the police, the outcome would have been very different. Dave would have been waiting at the house to meet Peggy when she arrived with Gabriella. It was probably the sight of the patrolling police car, the result of my alert, that had deterred him.

We told George about the note that had been pushed through the letterbox demanding we throw the package and letter out of the window. We told him too about Dave Smith and Peggy Browne coming to the house together later, claiming to be B&B owners who had been asked by one of their guests, Captain John Smith, to pick up his wrongly addressed mail, namely a package and a letter.

'Well,' George said, shaking his head, 'the hunt is unfortunately still on. I can see why Dick wanted you away from the house until this mess is all sorted out. I wonder now if somehow the quest for the package and letter has followed you here.'

'Oh, there's no doubt about that,' I said, and went on to tell him about the overheard lunchtime conversation between Jim and Sheila.

'It turns out that Sheila is Ron and Mick's sister. Jim, her husband, is originally from this area so they decided to come here this year for their holiday. By pure chance they happened to sit at a table next to ours in a restaurant and we overheard their conversation. That's how we discovered that they have been asked to look out for a blue Beetle which was thought to be in the Bungay area.'

'An older model blue Beetle,' Gabriella couldn't resist adding. She really can be a cat!

'Anyway,' I continued, ignoring my sister, 'we left the restaurant without waiting for dessert and rushed back here to hide the Beetle because we'd left it sitting out on the driveway in full view of the road.'

George turned to his mother and grinned. 'So it's Aunt Aggie's old blue Beetle that you have hidden in your garage, Mum!'

'Yes, don't you think we hid it well?'

'Suspiciously well! Think about it, anyone seeing your expensive new Audi sitting outside might well wonder why it hasn't been put in the garage, especially at night. Anyway, I can take care of that. Just excuse me a minute.'

He went out of the room with his phone in his hand. When he returned, he said, 'Right, that's done. Now, let's consider how Ron and Mick knew you were coming to Bungay. Did you tell anyone you were coming here or arrange for mail to be forwarded or leave a note anywhere saying where to find you in an emergency?'

'No, none of those things. We didn't decide to come to Bungay until after we left the house. Richard phoned and practically ordered us to leave your aunt's house immediately, so we just grabbed a few necessities, jumped in the car and drove off.'

'So you didn't tell Dick you were coming here?'

'No, he told us not to contact him and he hasn't contacted us, so we haven't been able to tell him where we are or anything about Sheila and Ron looking for the Beetle.'

'I did try to call him after we overheard their conversations,' I interposed, 'even though he told us not to, because we thought it was important. Anyway, as Gabby told you, he hasn't called back so far. Maybe you would have better luck calling him.'

'Leave it to me,' George replied. Again, he left the room.

34

I wasn't expecting anything more to happen right away so settled back to my book. George returned to the living room and went to look out of the window.

Gabriella said, 'I wish I'd known there would be three of us for dinner when I went shopping this morning. What would you both say to lamb chops? I've got plenty of mint in the garden to make mint sauce. I'll nip up to the butchers right away. Do either of you want me to bring anything else in while I'm out?'

Lamb chops sounded good to me.

Before I could say so, George cut in, 'Make do with what you already have in, Mum. I need you here.'

He needed Gabriella to stay home? Now that was intriguing.

'The first thing I need you to do is to get your Audi off the drive. Go and park it out on the road but well clear of the gate. By the way, is your garage door opener in the car?'

'Yes, I always keep it in the car, but ... '

'Bring it back with you.'

'But George, why ... '

'Please hurry Mum, I'll explain later.'

Gabriella bustled out importantly to do as she was bid. George now turned to me.

'Aunt Aggie, I need the Beetle key. Do you have it?'

'It's here in my purse.' I had already guessed by this time that there was a scheme afoot to remove the Beetle, so was ready with the key. I handed it to him.

Gabriella returned and gave George her clicker. He thanked her and spoke into his mobile, after which he had further instructions for us.

'Right Mum, now I'd like you to go and open your front door as wide as it'll go. When you've done that, go out and stand out on the footpath in front of the gate. A large furniture van will be coming along the road soon. When you see it, wave your arms madly and signal that this is the house to come to. Make sure that any people out there or any passing traffic see you signalling to the van. Then I want you to come back to the house and stand in the open doorway. Aunt Aggie, you stay here out of sight for the moment. OK both of you?'

We nodded. George and I stood well back from the window to watch while Gabriella opened her front door wide and then went out to the end of her drive.

It wasn't long before she started to wave her arms and signal. A large furniture van with 'Safest Furniture Delivery' written on its side slowed to a halt outside the gate. Gabriella walked briskly back to the house and took up her position at the open front door. The van maneuvered into position, then reversed carefully down the driveway, coming to a halt with its rear doors in front of the garage.

Three men got out. One went straight to the front door carrying a clipboard. He handed this to Gabriella who was ready and waiting for him. Meanwhile, the other two men opened the doors at the back of the van and lowered a ramp to the ground. The first man then went back to the van and disappeared up the ramp. He emerged carrying a heavy old-fashioned rocking chair, which he seemed to be holding very awkwardly and staggered with it towards the front door. I wondered why one of the other two men didn't go to help him with it. Halfway to the door he tripped and lost his balance, falling sideways between two of Gabriella's beautiful hydrangea shrubs and landed on the lawn, pinned down by the rocking chair. It seemed to me that he made rather more noise and fuss than necessary disentangling himself from under the chair but eventually he righted himself and carried it slowly and carefully into the house. I watched and saw him come out of the house again and go to the van. I wondered if there was more furniture to come, but he climbed straight up into the cab and the van drove off.

I had been so intrigued watching his antics with the rocking chair that I had completely missed whatever it was that the other two men were up to. I had of course kept my ears open for the sound of the Beetle being revved up in Gabriella's garage so that it could be driven up the ramp into the furniture van, but I had heard nothing to suggest this had happened. Mission failure, I supposed. Pity.

'I really hoped that furniture van had come for the Beetle,' I said ruefully to George. 'And all it did was bring a rocking chair.'

'That's what everybody was meant to think,' George grinned, looking like the cat that got the cream. 'The rocking chair delivery was a decoy to focus attention away from the van. It got your attention, didn't it? You see we didn't want an audience while the car was being loaded into the van.'

'You're telling me the Beetle's gone?' I wasn't entirely convinced. 'But George, I listened for the engine starting up. I know the sound well, and I have to tell you I didn't hear it. Are you sure the car actually made it into the van?'

'Don't worry, the Beetle's definitely gone. You didn't hear the engine because we didn't drive it into the van, we winched it in.' He grinned again. 'And it definitely won't be coming back to Bungay so it's up to you now to decide whether you want us to take it to Scotland or to the scrapheap. I'd strongly advise the latter. That old Beetle is now a marked car in two countries!'

'I agree, Aggie,' Gabriella nodded earnestly. 'In any case, that Beetle is long past its sell by date. I've been suggesting you get a new car for ages.'

I looked from one to the other.

'That's all very well,' I said, 'but I need a car, and the Beetle is in perfectly good running order. I haven't got money to burn, you know. I certainly couldn't afford a lovely Audi like yours.'

'What if you got a really good trade-in price on it, Aunt Aggie?'

George's eyes were sparkling. He was really enjoying persuading me to replace the Beetle. He can be quite like his mother sometimes.

'What if you got a much better trade in than you expected?' he persisted.

'George, you know as well as I do that all they do is look at the age of the car and consult a book for the trade-in price.'

'I doubt that trade-in price records go that far back, Aunt Aggie,' he said with a smirk. 'That car of yours came out of the ark.'

Gabriella, who can be sensitive sometimes, intervened. 'Aggs, if you had your choice of a new car tomorrow, and cost didn't come into it, what would you choose?'

'Oh, that's easy,' I said. 'If I could afford it I'd breeze right into the twenty-first century with one of those new BMW electric cars. They're so ugly, they're cute. I think they're called an i3. You need to have an electric charger fitted in your garage so you can keep them charged up. I've read all about them. I'll tell you what, Gabs. While I'm here, you and I could go round some car showrooms together.'

'It's a good idea to look at new cars while you're here,' George said carefully. 'But whatever you do, don't be tempted to buy one while you're here. You don't want to set off for Scotland by yourself in a brand new car that you haven't had time to get used to. Glitches can appear in new cars and you don't want that to happen on the motorway.'

I ignored George's fatuous remarks. I have driven cars since before he was born.

He stayed only another day after the furniture van came for my Beetle, spending much of his time on his telephone, tantalisingly out of earshot. I finally asked him if he had managed to contact Richard, and if so, was there was any prospect of my going home yet, but he was vague and evasive. He told me not to worry, just enjoy my holiday with my sister. Dick, he said, would call as soon as he was sure it was safe for me to go back.

After George left, I told Gabriella that although he had engineered the removal of my Beetle brilliantly, replacing it was actually none of his business. I also wondered whether he had passed on my request to Richard to contact me, since I still hadn't had a call from him. She got very defensive and told me George had important work to do and I shouldn't bother him with trivia. Now I don't know how asking a simple question constitutes bothering anybody and my question certainly wasn't trivia, but in the interests of peace I let it go. Gabriella always did have a blind spot regarding George.

'Don't get me wrong,' I told her. 'I'm very fond of George. I was truly grateful to him for getting my Beetle out of your garage and away from Bungay, and the furniture van and rocking chair decoy was absolutely brilliant. It's just that I'm frustrated at not hearing from Richard. I want to know that my house is still intact and I'd like some kind of projection as to when I can go home. Not that I'm not enjoying being here with you,' I hastened to add. 'I just wondered if there was any news.'

35

'You know what, Aggie,' Gabriella said the following morning, 'I've really neglected my garden lately. What with coming up to Scotland and then tootling round Suffolk with you this last week, I've not been out there enough and the weeds are taking over.'

I asked her if she had tried those little granules you can buy to spread on the garden to prevent weeds germinating after you've put in your plants. Gabriella was indignant.

'Chemicals! Not in my garden! My garden is organic!'

I didn't think it was the time to share the information that I sprinkle the granules shamelessly to cut down on weeding.

'What a good thing you're still here,' Gabriella continued. 'If we work together we should soon be able to get the front garden tidied up and then the back shouldn't take more than a couple of days.'

I sighed. I wasn't going to win that one. Gabriella had given her time unstintingly to help me, so helping her to catch up on her gardening was the least I could do. I would try to do it cheerfully.

'Just so long as you've got some decent gardening gloves for me to wear,' I said, forcing a smile to cover up my lack of enthusiasm.

'Wonderful!' Gabriella replied happily. 'Now that George has gone we can really get down to things. I'll tell you what, though. Before we start on the flower beds, let's get all those cuttings out of the garage window. They're not needed there now that the Beetle has gone and one of them could accidentally fall onto my Audi. Let me back it out and then we'll take the plants back to their shelf outside the kitchen window. Some of them will be ready for planting out soon. In fact, I'll check them to see if any are ready. That's something else you could help me with.'

The precious plants had to be carried carefully from the garage to the back of the house and placed on their shelf under the kitchen window one at a time. We had almost finished when we heard a voice coming from the driveway.

'Coo-ee! Hello-o!'

It was Sheila coming down the drive. She appeared to be alone.

Gabriella murmured. 'Leave this to me, I know just how to handle it.'

Turning to Sheila, she beamed. 'Marvellous! Just what we need, another pair of hands! Put on a pair of gloves, Sheila. You'll find them in that box by the door. We're carrying these cuttings outside. They've had long enough behind glass. Then we're going to weed the flowerbeds. We can use all the help we can get. Do you think Jim would like to come along and help too?'

Sheila looked horrified. She made no move towards the glove box.

'Oh, I don't think I'd be much use,' she faltered. 'I'm not a gardener at all.'

'Oh dear,' Gabriella gave an exaggerated sigh. 'I was really hoping you could help. Are you quite sure you don't want to try your hand? We can easily teach you.'

'No, really.' Sheila began to back away.

'Well, what about Jim?' Gabriella persisted. 'A lot of men love to garden. Why don't you go and ask him if he'd like to come along and help?'

Gabriella grinned as Sheila hurried off. We did not expect to see her again.

We finished moving the plants outside and she left the garage door open for easy access to gardening tools. We decided to start by pulling up weeds in the rose border which stretched along the driveway and at the same time remove rose heads that had finished flowering. We agreed that Gabriella should start by the house and I would work down from the gate end.

I became aware of voices along the footpath outside.

'No, I'm not going back in there. Honestly, they tried to get me to put on some gardening gloves. I couldn't believe it.'

'Are you sure there was nothing in the garage?'

'Nothing unless you count a load of useless plants and a box of gardening gloves. You can look and see for yourself. The door's open. And by the way, the car on the drive is a red Audi.'

'Does it look brand new? She could have traded in the Beetle.'

'Newish, but not brand new if the registration's anything to go by. It needs a good wash anyway. I dare say those two old girls think a lot more about their garden than they do about their car. You know Jim, I don't think we're going to find that old blue Beetle here. We shouldn't waste any more of our holiday on it. In fact, that's what I told Mam when I called her after breakfast. I said we're wasting our time.'

'What did she say to that?'

'She said Ron thinks it must be here because it isn't there.'

'Didn't you tell her to tell him that it isn't here either?'

'Yes I did, but she said he wants us to keep looking because it's important.'

'Didn't you tell her we've only two more days of our holiday left?'

'Yes.'

'Well you'd better call her back and tell her that we've looked all over Bungay and there was only one place we thought it could be hidden but you saw inside the place today and it was empty, so we're not looking for it any more.'

'You were the one that thought it might be there. I never did.'

'Yes you did, you said so last night. Anyway, did you ask those two old girls about it?'

'Of course I didn't ask them about it. I'm not stupid. I could see that the garage was empty. I'll tell you though, when they asked me if I wanted to help them do some gardening I couldn't get away quick enough.'

'Did they offer to pay you?'

'No.'

'Greedy bitches!'

We didn't see Sheila and Ron again. They could have brought havoc to Gabriella's quiet life in Bungay if they had seen my blue Beetle there and reported it to Ron and Mick. I said a silent thank you to George.

We worked daily in Gabriella's garden. It would have stayed weed free if only I'd had the duplicity to sprinkle anti-weed granules when she wasn't around. I was certainly tempted but in the end couldn't bring myself do it. Dedicated organic gardener that she is, Gabriella would have been mortified, so I dutifully did my daily stint in the garden with as much grace as I could muster while I waited with increasing anxiety for Richard to call.

When at last the call did come it took me by surprise. It was only seven-thirty in the morning and Gabriella and I were still having breakfast.

'Angelina! How are you?'

'Fine, thank you Richard. Are you calling to tell me it's all right to go home now?'

'Er, yes.'

'You seem a little hesitant. Is something wrong?'

'No, no, nothing's wrong. I'll tell you all about it on the way home.'

Now that sounded odd because I had imagined Richard to be still in Scotland. He certainly wouldn't travel all the way to Bungay just to escort me home. So where was he now?

'Well, I definitely want to hear all about it,' I said cautiously. 'But Richard, where are you calling from?'

'Oh, I suppose I didn't tell you, I've been in London. George told me I should allow three hours to drive to Bungay. That seems an awfully long time to me. I'm sure I'll be able to do it in less.'

'I've never actually driven here from London, let me ask Gabriella.'

Gabriella confirmed that driving from London to Bungay could take three hours if the traffic is jugged up, but two and a half hours would be more usual.

'Right,' said Richard when I relayed this, 'can you be ready to leave by, say, nine o'clock?'

How could I turn down such an offer? I didn't bother to correct his maths on the time estimate.

'I'll be ready,' I said. 'And thanks, Richard.'

It didn't take long to collect my things because I had brought so little with me, so I was soon packed and ready to go. What I did want to do, though, was to finish the book I was reading and leave it in Bungay rather than take it with me. I had got as far as the last but one chapter and I reckoned I had a good hour in which to finish it. I put my purse, travel bag and coat by the door and settled down in my favourite chair.

'Aggie!' Gabriella shrieked just after nine o'clock, 'I thought you said Richard was in London. He can't have been, not unless he and his car rode here on a magic carpet!'

She was looking out of the window onto the driveway.

'What's all the fuss about, Gabs? I answered, not looking up. 'Richard won't be here for another hour at least. I know he said nine o'clock but obviously he should have said ten.'

'Well, you'd better come and see for yourself because I'm watching either Richard Carter or his twin brother getting out of a car right now.'

That got me to the window in a hurry. And sure enough there he was, dear handsome Richard. He seemed to glow with the sun shining on his silvering hair. I'd never been so happy to see him! He spotted us waving out of the window and waved back. Gabriella rushed out immediately to meet him with me following a close second. She flung her arms round his neck joyfully. He gave her a quick, friendly peck on the cheek then gently disengaged himself and turned to envelop me in a long, lasting bear hug. Oh, how wonderful it felt! I could have stayed there all day. As we broke apart though, I realised how my rapturous greeting must have appeared to Gabriella, compared with her own perfunctory peck. I looked anxiously to see if she was upset, because my sister can get quite jealous. She had gone indoors. Not a good sign.

Richard took care of the situation, however. He can be amazingly sensitive.

'Gabriella,' he called, 'I've got something here for you. It's something George asked me to bring specially for you. It's quite a large box, I'd better carry it in for you. I don't know what's in it but he said it's something you will enjoy.'

That did the trick. She bustled out of the house, unable to wait to see what her precious George had sent, and for that matter neither could Richard and I. We followed her to the kitchen table and watched her carefully unpack several different packages of spring bulbs for her garden.

'Oh, Aggie.' She was overjoyed. 'Just look. What a pity you won't be here to help me plant them. I know just where I'm going to put them. Anyway, these will keep me busy after you've gone. You know I'm going to miss having you here.'

I hugged her. I was going to miss her too, but I knew Richard and I should set off right away if we were to get home that day.

'We'll have to get off, Gabs,' I told her. 'But

thanks for everything. You've been marvellous. I'll call you this evening to let you know I'm home.'

'Drive safely,' she called after us as we left.

36

The reason Richard arrived an hour before expected was that he was already on the way to Bungay when he called us. He decided it was too early to call before he left London so he set off and called en route when he thought we would probably be up and about.

As we drove north he told me the intelligence services had discovered that the information leak George was sent to Scotland to investigate was only one part of a multifaceted international espionage system. More arrests had been made at the military base and the Scottish connection was now considered dead. Richard had been called urgently to London to assist an investigative committee. That was why he hustled Gabriella and myself away from Dunoon. He wouldn't be there to protect us.

Dear, dear Richard! I felt a lovely warm glow. I forgave him everything.

George had been called to assist the committee too. He was abroad at the time but managed to join them shortly before the close of the meeting. It was he that suggested that instead of taking a flight home, Richard might prefer to rent a car and drive me back to Scotland.

'Naturally,' he told me gallantly, 'I jumped at the idea.'

Hmm, so that's what George had in mind when he advised me not to buy another car immediately. Dear George, I forgave him everything too!

'Naturally,' I replied in the same light tone, 'I'm delighted to have you chauffeur me home. But before anything else, Richard, there's something I should mention in case you're unaware of it.'

'Oh? Don't worry, Angelina, everything's quiet at home now. Dave Smith was taken in for questioning and he couldn't wait to point the finger away from himself so we got the civilian end as well as the military. It's all cleared up now. Nothing to worry about.'

'Including Ron and Mick?'

'Ron and Mick? Those two? Don't worry about them. They're out of the picture. They were never part of the espionage group. They were just a couple of heavies hired by Dave to find George's package and letter.'

'Ah well,' I said, pausing for effect, 'as it happens, I can tell you exactly where they went.'

Richard paused too for a moment. 'I'm guessing,' he said, 'you're going to tell me they went to York. Yes, like you I remembered the time we listened in on their conversation outside your house, when they talked about York and their mother's birthday party. We enjoyed that, didn't we? And then, of course, George told me how you and Gabriella met their sister Sheila and her husband, who were from York too. He also told me how he spirited your blue Beetle away in a furniture van because you and Gabriella discovered that Ron had asked his sister to look for it in the Bungay area.'

'Well, doesn't all that suggest they've gone to York?'

'Suggest yes, but the fact is, they haven't gone to York, at least not so far. We've been watching out for them.'

'Richard,' I spoke carefully, 'first you told me that Ron and Mick have disappeared but it doesn't matter because they're not important. Then you tell me that you've been watching out for them. Isn't that a bit of a contradiction?'

'Not really, it's just a matter of tying up loose ends. Don't worry.'

'I am worried. Didn't George tell you that Sheila and Jim were expecting to be paid by Ron and Mick for locating my blue Beetle? And we know that Ron and Mick were expecting to be paid by Dave Smith for finding the package and letter. They're looking for my car now, so they must think that's where they're hidden. I just bet Ron and Mick don't know Dave Smith has been caught, and that's why they're still looking for the car, still expecting be paid for finding that package and letter.'

'Mm, I suppose you could be right.'

'And you told me they're not in York, so now I'm wondering if maybe they're heading for Bungay. Oh Richard, I suddenly have this awful feeling Gabriella could be in danger.'

'I suppose it's a remote possibility. Look, we can go back if only to put your mind at rest. I'll just have to find somewhere to turn the car round, then Bungay, here we come!'

Richard turned into a farm gateway, got out of the car and spoke on his mobile. His expression became serious. Getting back in the car, he started the engine. 'Have you got your mobile handy, Angelina?'

'Yes, it's here in my purse.'

'Call your sister now and tell her we're coming back. Tell her to lock her house and go straight to the nearest pub and stay there. Tell her to get coffee and a snack at the pub if she's hungry while she waits for us, but on no account must she go home. Emphasise that she must stay there until we arrive.'

Gabriella was busy with her spring bulbs. She was not at all pleased to be told to drop everything and go to the pub for no obvious reason.

'Just trust me, Gabs.' I pleaded. 'Richard is very worried He's just been on the phone. He thinks Ron and Mick may be on the way to your house.'

'That's rubbish. We know they're going to York. Didn't you tell him?'

'Please, Gabs, the situation's changed since

he talked on the phone.' I had a sudden inspiration. 'It could have been George he was talking to.'

'George?'

'Possibly.'

I had no idea who Richard had talked to of course, but mention of George did the trick. She agreed to go straight to the pub and wait there.

'You know, Richard,' I said to him after I finished the call to Gabriella, 'there's something else that's been worrying me ever since we ran into Sheila and Jim. I just can't figure out what made Ron and Mick think I was going to Bungay. We rushed off in such a hurry, Gabs and I didn't even decide where to go until after we left Dunoon.'

'No, that's something we need to find out.'

'I mentioned it to George. He may have forgotten though.'

'I don't think George would forget. More likely he did investigate but didn't feel it was important enough to report back to you.'

Another example of George's high-handedness! He is very like his mother sometimes. I spoke rather more sharply than poor Richard deserved. 'Well it's important to me!'

Richard smiled gently and patted my hand. 'Don't let it upset you, he's very good at his job.'

'I know,' I sighed, ' I'm sorry, I know George is good at his job.'

37

We got back to Bungay and headed straight for the pub to meet Gabriella. Imagine our alarm as we turned into the pub car park to see the brake lights of a tan SUV right outside the door. Ron and Mick got out of the vehicle and went inside the pub.

'Just keep calm and keep your head down,' Richard said, parking across from the SUV. 'I'd like you to stay here in the car. It'll be better if I go in by myself. They don't know me. You can watch through the driving mirror, but, whatever you do, keep your head down if you see them.'

'But I have to go in with you,' I protested. 'I can't leave Gabriella to face those two thugs alone.'

'She won't be alone. I'll be there, and there are sure to be other people around too. She won't come to any harm in the pub. Just trust me on this. Please.'

I wasn't at all happy but had to concede that Richard was right. I stayed put in the car and watched through the driving mirror as he strode across the car park. When I saw him trip on something near the pub door and land against the side of the SUV I thought it just served him right, then chided myself for such a mean thought. Anyway, he couldn't have been hurt because he pulled himself up holding on to the door and was immediately back on his feet again. I made a mental note to tell Gabriella to remind the landlord to make a safety check on the ground outside the pub door.

What happened subsequently inside the pub was reported to me later by Gabriella. She had been watching anxiously for Richard and me, so saw Ron and Mick as soon as they came through the door. Her senses on high alert, she watched and listened.

Ron went straight to the bar and ordered two beers. He said casually to the barman, 'I'm looking for a friend who lives in Bungay.'

'Oh yes,' said the barman, 'and who would that be?'

'A lady. You might know her.'

'What's her name?'

'Maud.'

'Don't know of any Mauds round here. Plenty of Janes and Susans and Tiffanys and names like that but no Mauds that I know of. What does she look like?'

'Er, about as tall as my brother here,' he indicated Mick, 'and her hair ...'

Before he could comment on my hair he was interrupted by Mick, who had been looking round the room while his brother talked to the barman.

'Look Ron,' he pointed across the room to Gabriella, 'there she is, over there.'

Ron threw some money on the bar counter, picked up the two beers and followed Mick to the table where she sat, not looking at all pleased and still wearing her gardening gear. Her gardening gloves lay on the table next to an empty coffee cup and a couple of empty biscuit wrappers.

The barman turned his attention to Richard. 'What can I get you, sir?'

'Orange juice please, I'm driving.'

As Richard carried his drink to the table next to Gabriella he put his finger to his lips and shook his head slightly, signalling her to ignore him.

Meanwhile, without asking if she minded, Ron took one of the empty chairs at Gabriella's table and Mick took another. Ron looked menacingly at her.

'Excuse me, luv. We need to have a little talk.'

Gabriella glared back at him. 'I'm certainly not your love. I don't know who you are. I didn't invite you to sit at my table and I can't imagine what you think we need to talk about. What do you want?'

'Only to talk to you.'

'If you want to talk to me you'll have to make an appointment. I can write the number down for you.'

'Don't be daft, lady. We can talk 'ere.'

'No, I' m afraid we can't. I only see patients in my clinic.'

'What clinic?'

'Are you sure you're talking to the right person? You do know that I'm a consultant psychiatrist, don't you? And as I told you, I don't see patients out of the clinic.'

'Come off it, luv. Who do you think you're fooling. A doctor, dressed like that? You're just an old biddy come in 'ere for a rest from 'er gardening.'

'She were better dressed in York though, Ron,' Mick pointed out.

'Aye, she were.' Ron looked more carefully at Gabriella. 'We saw you in York.'

'I was in York about three weeks ago,' she agreed. 'Did you have an appointment with me at my clinic there? Maybe you were seen by one of my colleagues. I'm sure I would have remembered seeing you.'

Ron was getting impatient. His voice rose a decibel. 'Don't be so daft, woman! What were you doing in York?'

The barman, who had been watching this interchange with growing anxiety, now came quickly across to Gabriella's table.

'Dr Chester, are these men bothering you?'

Ron and Mick stared at Gabriella, then at the barman and then back to her. Ron shuffled to his feet.

'Sorry doctor, my mistake. We thought you

were someone else.'

'Yes, sorry doctor.' Mick echoed and rose too. 'You look like someone else. Sorry to have bothered you.'

Gabriella smiled benignly at them. 'A lot of us look like someone else, you know. I dare say there are other men that look just like you do. Don't give it another thought. By the way, I don't think I gave you the clinic number, did I? Would you like me to write it down for you?'

'Thank you, ma'am, we won't be needing it.'

The two men hurried towards the pub door, leaving their beer untouched on the table.

I had been watching the door through the car mirror and saw Ron and Mick hurry out, climb into their car and drive off.

Richard emerged from the pub a couple of minutes later.

'Did you see which way they went?' he asked.

'Yes,' I told him. 'I watched them go. They turned left and Gabriella's house is to the right.'

'Good,' he said. 'We'd better go and check the house before telling her it's OK to go home.'

We stopped along the road in front of Gabriella's house and waited see if the SUV came back that way. After about ten minutes, with no sign of the SUV, Richard went to check the house for signs of a break-in. He returned to report there were no forced doors, broken windows or any other evidence that Ron and Mick had been there before going to the pub. He took out his mobile and dialled a number, listened and smiled.

'All clear!' he told me. 'And they're headed away from Bungay.'

'I do hope so.'

'They're gone.'

'How can you be sure?'

'I'm putting this on speaker. Listen.'

I listened, and to my surprise heard the now familiar voices of Ron and Mick. From the gist of their conversation they were leaving. Who, I wondered had bugged their car? Then I remembered seeing Richard trip and steady himself against the SUV in the pub car park before he followed Ron and Mick in. He must have planted the bug then. Hmm! Clever Richard!

'I thought a listening device would have to be inside the car. How on earth did you get one in through a closed door?'

'The window was open. Serendipity.'

The voices were somewhat blurred by the engine noise but it was still possible to make out what Ron and Mick were saying.

' ... Bloody wild goose chase if you ask me.'

'It were your idea to come, not mine. I said all along it would be a waste of time. Sheila told us there weren't no bloody blue Beetle 'ere. You should 'ave listened to 'er, but no, you 'ad to know best, you silly bugger, just like you always do. All we found was that bloody psychic look alike."

'She said psychiatrist, not psychic.'

'Same difference. Bloody fruitcake if you ask me. I think she liked you though, Ron. Wanted you to make an appointment to see 'er again, didn't she? Offered 'er number twice an' all. Wonder if she 'as a crystal ball and dresses up in all them scarves.'

'Don't be so bloody thick. A psychiatrist is a doctor, for folks as need their heads examined.'

'Aye well, that's what you need, isn't it, bringing us all this way for nowt. All because you found those bits o' paper with Bungay and Maud written on 'em.'

'Those bits o' paper were part of a torn-up letter. You saw it. That were detective work, that were, Mick. Detectives always look in wastepaper baskets for evidence. It's in all the books.'

'I didn't see you looking in any basket.'

'I tipped it out though, didn't I? Them bits of letter fell into my shoe. I found them when I went to bed that night. They call that kismet, Mick, kismet.'

''Ow do you make that out then?'

'Because I tipped out a whole lot of other torn bits of letters and things and some bits of cardboard and brown paper and stuff ... Oh, bloody 'ell, Mick! Bloody 'ell!'

'What's up?'

'Oh, Mick, she'd torn 'em up, 'adn't she. The silly bitch 'ad torn 'em up!'

'Torn what up?'

'That's why we couldn't find 'em. All this

time we've been looking for 'em and the silly bitch 'ad torn 'em up!'

'You don't mean she tore up them things we've been looking for? Oh, bloody 'ell, no wonder we couldn't find 'em. They weren't there, were they?'

'No, they bloody weren't. What a bloody farce. All that looking for nowt!'

'Aye, all for nowt. But 'ang on a minute Ron, I've just 'ad a thought.'

'Oh aye.'

'Dave doesn't know they're not there, does he? He doesn't know they got torn up and binned.'

''Course he doesn't know ... hey, and you know what?'

'What?'

'We're not going to tell him, are we? Right?'

'Right! I'll tell you what though.'

'What?'

'You're a genius, Ron, a bloody genius!'

'Aye, I am, and you know what else? It takes a genius to know when to call it a day. Dave bloody Smith can get someone else to work for him now.'

'What about us getting paid?'

'Aye well, that's not going to 'appen is it?'

'What makes you think that?'

'Because they're all torn up, that's why. There's nowt for Dave to get paid for. He was going to pay us for finding them and there's nowt to find.'

'Oh aye.'

'And I've been thinking. We've seen too much of 't bloody police while we've been working for Dave. It weren't him that nearly got caught those times, it were us. And our Mam tells me there's some new houses being built just outside York, a real big development. She said they're hiring workers. What do you say?'

'You're a genius, Ron, a bloody genius.'

It was finally time to tell Gabriella it was safe for her to go home. It was finally safe for me to go home too. And I was going home with Richard. My paper chase was over.

EPILOGUE

We did leave Bungay that day, but not until early afternoon because we took Gabriella home from the pub, where she had been marooned for a couple of hours, the monotony broken only by her brief contretemps with Ron and Mick. Richard was busy on the phone quite a while, presumably in connection with the day's events. Gabriella beckoned me to go down the garden with her.

She told me that during her time in the pub she had done a lot of thinking and now she wanted to apologise to me and clear the air. Sibling rivalry, she told me, could be a terrible thing and as a psychiatrist she should have known better. She had immediately recognised a strong mutual attraction between Richard and myself, but out of longstanding habit had seen it as something of a challenge and persuaded herself that a mild flirtation with Richard was fair game. She asked me to forgive her and promise that it would not come between us in the future.

She added that I might keep my eye out for any eligible brothers, cousins, friends or colleagues Richard might have. As she said, you never know your luck.

It occurred to me that Gabriella was not the only sister guilty of sibling rivalry, I have always liked to feel I hold the moral high ground, as befits a twin who is the elder by twenty minutes. I was saved from possibly unwise soul baring by Richard coming down the garden to tell me it was time to go. I hugged Gabriella and thanked her for being such a wonderful and understanding sister.

Because we were so late leaving Bungay we broke our journey overnight in York. Richard suggested York as a sort of catharsis for me, like getting back on a bicycle after falling off. For good measure, we stayed in the hotel by the river, the scene of Ron and Mick's futile search for the package and letter. Richard asked whether I would prefer one room or two. I told him there was really no need to waste money. Then he asked if I had a preference for twin beds or double. I told him I had chosen the room so he could choose the bed(s).

There is no need to spell out further details of our night in the hotel, they are more than adequately described over several pages in many of the books available in bookstores and on library shelves, fiction and non-fiction. How about that for the elder twin holding the moral high ground?

Richard and I are currently living in my refurbished house in Dunoon. His house next door is rented out. We have talked of selling both houses and moving elsewhere but so far haven't found anywhere else we would prefer to be.

Gabriella met her own beau the following summer but that's another, and somewhat complicated, story!

Printed in Great Britain
by Amazon